UNLUCKY BUMPKIN

SAM CHEEVER

ELECTRIC PROSE PUBLICATIONS

She's just a country girl who loves her dog...and her cat...and her pig. But a cold-blooded killer might suck the sweet right out of her bucolic little world.

Lance Lucklin has always had the luck of the Irish, though he's about as far from Irish as you can get. It is, after all, how he got his nickname, Lucky Lucklin. But it appears that his luck has run out in a big way. That's putting it mildly, I guess. Since Lucky just turned up dead, hanging from a tool hook at my family's auction business.

Was Lucky's death meant as a warning for me? Could this mean the return of an old villain? Will Hal and I be called on to help the local Deer Hollow police find a killer?

In the end, luck probably won't have much to do with the outcome. Luck can be made. And as death stalks the people I love, I'm fully prepared to force the hand of fate and create my own luck. Or die trying.

1

I stood in the gravel and stared past the high metal fence, topped with double rows of razor wire. The buildings in the distance were half shrouded in fog, their familiar lines softened in the mist. Somewhere inside the ten-foot-high fence, lost in the thick mist, the squat stone ranch house that had served as an office waited for me to step through the door and begin the process of closing down what had once been an integral part of my life. Shutting a door I'd never be able to open again, except through memories made less distinct by the passage of time.

The sign attached to the wide gates proclaimed the hundred-acre space as *Fulle-Proof Auctions*. The auction had been my family's business for decades, until my parents had been believed killed in the crash of a private plane at the back of our property. I'd since learned I hadn't lost them both, but the past the acres of gravel and assortment of metal buildings represented had died along with my father in that small plane.

Beside me, Caphy whined softly, no doubt sensing my sadness. It had been a tough decision to sell the place. My dad had loved the auction. He'd built it from a tiny farm auction to a business that took in equipment of all sizes from around the country and brought top dollar for quality offerings.

Selling it now would be like severing the final link with my dad. To me, it felt like cutting off a limb, leaving me bloodied, my memories set adrift in a mist not unlike the one surrounding Caphy and me at that moment.

But after much discussion, my mom and I had finally come to the only decision we could. The auction needed to be sold. My father wasn't coming back, and neither my mom nor I would be running the business. Sitting empty, it was just a liability. Besides, I'd been receiving nearly daily calls from people who wondered when the auction would live again.

There were people who'd counted on the service my father had once provided. It was time to let someone else provide it.

I shoved my heavy blonde hair off my face, fighting tears. "It's okay, Caphy girl. I'm just feeling a little sad."

She swiped a wide wet tongue over my hand and

gave her muscular tail a quick wag along the ground. But her green gaze told me she wasn't buying it. She always had been able to read me like a book.

Headlights flashed through the mist and skimmed over us, followed by the soft rumble of a car engine. A big car.

Tears burned my eyes. I bit back a sob.

He'd come.

Somewhere down deep, I'd known he would. Though he had to have driven most of the night to get there in time.

The big SUV pulled up next to my car and stopped, the lights flaring into the dense mist as the Greek god behind the wheel extinguished the engine. The door opened and he stepped out, hurrying around the car to wrap me in strong arms that were filled with the comfort he'd known I'd need. Despite my assurances that I was fine.

"Hey," he said, his voice rumbly against my ear as I pressed into him. He felt warm and solid in my arms. At six four, he was a foot taller than me and dark where I was light. His Greek heritage had given him thick shiny black hair that was swept straight back from a wide, unlined brow and curled softly at the top of his muscular neck. Even in the light of the SUV's headlights, his dark green gaze and wide, sensual mouth showed weariness.

I reached up and ran a finger gently over the razor-thin scar that ran from just in front of his left ear to the corner of his eye. "Hey," I responded. "You came."

"Of course."

Hal had been on special assignment in Tennessee when I'd told him what I'd planned. He'd asked me to wait, but I knew I had to do it fast, like yanking off a band-aid, or I might not have the will to do it at all. As it was, I'd been awake most of the night, wavering back and forth about my decision. I'd nearly called my realtor Madge Watson to cancel our appointment several times.

For more than one reason, she wouldn't have thanked me. The biggest one being the fact that it had been the wee hours of the morning when I'd plucked my cell off the bedside table and fought with myself not to dial.

"Is Madge here yet?" Hal asked. It was like he'd read my mind.

I shook my head. "She's not coming for a few hours. She needs to take pictures so she wants light." I wrinkled my nose. "And hopefully less fog."

He chuckled, one big hand rubbing my back in slow circles. "Did you bring boxes?"

"Some..."

He must have heard the struggle in my voice because he kissed the top of my head. "I brought some."

He knew me too well. Deep, deep down inside I was

pretty sure I was indulging in a bit of self-sabotage. I'd brought far fewer boxes than I knew I'd need. Reluctant to take the final step of boxing up my dad's stuff.

I sighed, nodding.

"You have the key?"

I dug into the pocket of my jeans and handed it to him. "I'll see you inside." Suddenly unwilling to watch him unlock the gate, I hurried around my car and slid inside after Caphy. The strange reluctance made me wonder how long I'd have stood there if Hal hadn't shown up.

I was thinking it would have been a while.

Headlights cutting pale circles over the empty gravel between the gate and the low-slung brick building, I drove slowly into the complex and parked in front of the office. I forced myself to climb out of the car as Hal parked beside me. Caphy disappeared into the fog, tail happily wagging. She'd always loved the auction lot, no doubt finding it a delicious abundance of scents and small skittering critters to harass.

Hal unlocked the door to the office as I stood staring off into the cloaking miasma, rubbing my arms. Sadness filled me at the sound of the door opening with a soft whoosh, stale air tumbling out to greet me.

It was really going to happen.

I was going to sell Fulle-Proof Auctions.

I'd be severing a huge chunk of my memories and my childhood along with it.

And I was pretty sure I'd be slicing off a chunk of my heart too.

I carefully boxed up the things in the outer office first, intending to store them in the attic at home until my mom had a chance to go through them. As Hal carried the last box out of the building, I stood in the center of the space, memories of hours spent playing there as a child rolling over me.

The sights and sounds of those carefree days, skewed by my childhood viewpoint and made more poignant through nostalgia, were like ghosts spinning through the room, long gone but never forgotten.

I'd perched in the dusty, threadbare armchair between the two office doors and played with my dolls, spinning tales of exciting adventures and happily ever afters until my mom yelled at me to go outside and play or, when I got a bit older, to do my homework.

The scarred wooden desk that dominated the outer office had been my favorite place to do my homework when the office manager, Betty, had gone home for the day. Thinking about the slightly overweight, middle-aged woman made me sad. I hadn't even known when she'd died a few weeks after the plane crash. I'd been too deep into my own grief to notice. And I'd had no inkling until recently that the two deaths might have even been connected. Recalling the kind-hearted woman who'd always brought me treats, that thought made me immeasurably sad.

The door opened and Hal came in, the early morning sunshine behind him. "Madge is here."

I rubbed my dusty hands on my jeans and nodded, my gaze sliding toward the two closed office doors. As I headed outside to meet the realtor, I couldn't help feeling at least a little relieved to get a short reprieve from the task ahead of me.

Packing up my parents' offices.

We found Madge snapping pictures outside the biggest structure. I was relieved to see that the bright sunshine had burned off the last of the fog, but its stark touch wasn't doing much to hide the fading and worn metal of the main auction building.

Madge turned as I walked up, giving me a smile. "Mornin'."

I smiled back. "Hey, Madge. What do you think? Should I invest the money in getting these buildings painted?" I hated to do that. It would cost me a small fortune. But, if it would help me get a better price for the auction, it might be worth doing.

"Let's hold off on that. I think I can maximize the

potential with the right angles and lighting. And to tell you the truth, this auction is a goldmine. I don't think you'll have any trouble selling it."

Her words should have made me feel better. But a small part of me hoped it didn't sell for a while. I needed a few months to wrap my head around letting it go. "Shall we go inside?"

Hal and I started forward without waiting for her response. Madge fell into step beside us. Hal pulled the massive doors of the main building open, and we stepped through.

The past roared over me, nearly taking me to my knees. Hal grabbed my elbow as tears filled my eyes. I stared at the rows of bleachers down the long sides of the enormous building, remembering how I'd played underneath them during the auctions. I'd spent hours clambering over, under and around them while my dad and Uncle Dev, my godfather and dad's lifelong best friend, had examined and discussed potential items for future auctions.

The sun formed perfect rectangles on the dusty ground, its light framed by clear sections of roof high above. The familiar smell, a mix of gasoline and sawdust, brought those days of adventure and endless possibilities back in a dizzying rush.

Hal bent his head to look me in the eyes. "Are you okay, honey?"

I sniffed, scraping the heel of my hand under my

eyes. "I'm fine. It's just been a while since I've been in here."

"The building's in great shape," said Madge. She was twenty yards away, walking down the wide center aisle and assessing the property. "You won't have to do anything with this, Joey."

I nodded, relieved.

She stopped near the end and pointed at a small door. "What's that?"

"The annex," I called out to her, setting off in her direction. "A mechanical room. Dad kept parts there in case something broke down on the day of an auction."

The "annex" was a second, smaller building built off the side of the main auction building and connected only by that small door. There was a larger, garage type door on the short side of the attached building so they could drive equipment into the annex for repairs. My father had always kept the mechanical room secured because the parts he kept inside tended to be worth a lot of money.

"You'll probably need to use the key," I told Hal as we joined Madge in front of the door.

Thank goodness my father'd had the foresight to key all the locks the same. A single key worked for everything. At the time, he'd said it was for expediency, but we'd both known it was because my mother always lost her keys. She could lose them walking from the front door to the car and never find them again.

It was a skill I luckily hadn't inherited.

Hal turned the key and the knob and shoved the door open.

We reared back in shock and revulsion.

"Ugh!" said Madge. "What is that?"

A foul stench I recognized all too well wafted out, sending us all stumbling back away from the door.

Death.

2

I rubbed my hands over my arms and watched from near the door as Deputy Arno Willager examined the corpse hanging from the corkboard on the wall.

Beside me, Hal's gaze was taking in the room, snapping mental pictures of the scene like the digital camera Arno wouldn't let him use.

I fought nausea, covering my nose and mouth and wishing the smell didn't feel like something alive. I was pretty sure it was growing on the back of my tongue like peach fuzz. I was afraid to swallow for fear the fuzz would grow down my throat.

Hal finally stopped cataloging the horrific scene of death and looked down at me, frowning. "Honey, you look thoroughly spooked. Why don't you go wait outside with Madge?"

The realtor had taken one look at the man

hanging from an oversized hook on the corkboard and run screaming from the room. I wouldn't have been surprised to find out she was still running, arms flailing around over her head and her screams shredding the morning quiet as she ran down the road in her sensible loafers and ill-fitting dark suit.

I shook my head. "I'm okay."

Hal squeezed my arm. "I'll be right back."

I watched him walk across the room. Deputy Arno Willager turned and frowned as Hal approached, stopping just beyond the area the cop had determined was the crime scene. Though about the same age, the two men couldn't be more different.

Lean and attractive, with brown eyes and a permanently creased brow, Arno was blonde where Hal was dark. Arno perpetually acted as if he carried the weight of the world on his shoulders, where Hal always seemed to take things in stride.

But each in his own way was strong, trustworthy and kind.

And they were fast becoming good friends.

It hadn't taken the police long after their arrival to figure out that the killer and the dead man had entered through the larger door at the end of the building, probably using an electronic opener that they'd somehow rekeyed to work that particular door.

The police and Hal had mapped the killer's

likely path from the door to the built-in tool bench on the outside wall. It looked to me like the killer had grabbed a hammer and beaten the dead guy with it.

Brutally.

From the deep, bloody holes in the victim's head and neck, I was pretty sure the killer had used the claws on the back of the hammer rather than the head of the tool to commit his heinous act.

I cleared my throat, unable to shake the feeling that death still coated it as I swallowed. I pushed the obsessive thought away, using my other senses to assess what I was seeing. Dusty footprints led from the big door to the tool bench. Gravel dust. There were two sets of prints, their differences easily discerned. One set was oversized, the pattern smeared, but where it was clear, the tread was segmented and chunky. I decided it was probably some kind of work boot. The second set of prints was narrow and pointed, with smooth soles. I looked at the dead man's fancy cowboy boots and realized those prints had to be his.

He wore dark jeans that had probably been spotless before they'd gotten sprayed with blood and... other things. His plaid cotton shirt looked like it might have been new, the fabric crisp and bright. His longish blond hair was compressed in a bowl shape on his head as if he'd been wearing a hat, and curved upward beneath the compression.

From where I was standing, the big yellow tractor in the center of the room hid half of the floor and wall from my view. I was guessing the man's hat was lying on the floor over there somewhere. His head was bowed, his chin resting on his chest in death, and I was glad.

I didn't want to see his face. Or the last moments of his death reflected in his eyes.

Hal turned and walked back to me, his steps brisk. "Come on, honey. Let's get out of here."

I shook my head. "I want to know who it is."

"I'll tell you what I know in the car."

Arno broke away from the other cops and strode over, his expression dark. "I'm guessing he's been dead about forty-eight hours. His name's Lance Lucklin, Joey. People call him Lucky. He's a gambler. Likes the casinos. He's been thrown out of a few for trying to cheat. Do you know him?"

I tried the name on for size and decided I'd never heard it before. Shaking my head, I asked, "Should I?"

Arno shrugged. "There's got to be a reason he ended up here, at Fulle-Proof Auctions."

"Well, when you figure that out, I hope you'll tell me. If this has something to do with my mom..." I let the words drift away, trusting the cop to understand the gist of my concern.

Arno frowned. "That thought had occurred to me too. I'll look into it. But I don't think Lucky

Lucklin is big-time enough to be involved with Garland Medford."

Medford was a wealthy businessman in Indianapolis who reputedly had ties to drugs, sex-trafficking, and murder. He'd paid someone to kill my parents because he believed they'd taken something from him. Two somethings actually. Money and a girlfriend, who'd been misidentified in the crash as my mother. Unfortunately, the contract killer Medford had hired to take out my parents was still out there somewhere.

And he knew my mother was alive.

Medford and his killer were the reason my mother had gone into hiding.

It still rankled that neither had faced charges. Medford because he was way too slick to have anything pinned on him. And Johnston, the paid assassin, because he'd light-footed it out of Deer Hollow, leaving his wife to pay for their crimes.

"I have no idea what connection Lucky could have to Medford," Arno said again, as if mulling it over in his mind. "But I'll dig into it."

I nodded. "If we're done here, I should get Caphy home, and Ethel needs to be fed," I told Hal. We'd locked Caphy in the office after finding the body. Arno wouldn't have thanked us if the nosy pitty had tromped all over his crime scene.

He nodded. Ethel Squeaks was our miniature pot-bellied pig. We'd gotten Ethel at Christmas time, adopting her when her beloved owner had been killed. She was a joy and we both doted on her. But if she didn't eat every few hours, her comfortable little porcine world came crashing down around her big, twitchy ears. She could be very dramatic in her retaliation. The last time we'd gotten home late to give her a midday snack, we'd found all of my bed pillows and blankets mounded up inside the tent, her pudgy little body stretched rebelliously in the middle of them.

Happy to be home, I stepped through my front door and looked down as a bright yellow ball rolled across the tiles, bumping against my boots.

Ethel stood in the entryway, tail spinning and bright black eyes shining with happiness at seeing us.

Hal gave the ball a tap with his foot, sending it past Ethel into the kitchen.

Caphy bounded through the front door, tail wagging in happy anticipation, as Ethel Squeaks spun and attempted to outrun her to the kitchen. They both hit the door at the same time and slammed to a halt as they wedged there.

I laughed, having seen the exact same thing several times before.

Ethel let loose a barrage of squeaks, more than earning her name, and managed to be the first one to wriggle free, her tiny hooves cutting the distance to the ball as Caphy dug in and flew after her.

A beat later, the ball came shooting back out and Caphy slammed it with a paw that sent it into the living room.

Hal closed the door and took my coat from me. "Those two are a clown show."

Laughing, I tugged off my boots, leaving them on the mat by the door. "I just hope they don't knock that lamp over aga..."

A familiar thump told me it was too late. "And there it went."

"I'll go settle them down."

I nodded. "I'll fix Ethel's lunch and get Caphy a snack."

Heading toward the kitchen, I called out to the resident feline, wondering if the ruckus on the main level had sent her to one of her favorite upstairs hidey holes. "LaLee? Here, kitty, kitty."

Caphy and Ethel, having matching appetites as well as a shared love of balls, both came running when they heard the refrigerator door opening.

Ethel slid to a dainty stop a few feet away and stood staring at me, tail twirling and snout quivering with interest. I set an assortment of fruit and raw veggies on the counter and bent to scratch her between her big ears. "Hello, pretty girl. Are you having a good day?"

Ethel squealed exuberantly. She was probably yelling at me to hurry up and feed her. I chose to believe she was telling me how much fun she'd been having.

The pibl flew across the kitchen, throwing on the brakes too late, as usual. She skidded across the tile and slammed into the back of my legs.

I nearly went down, only keeping my feet by grabbing the countertop. "Caphy, girl! Settle down." I frowned, rubbing my calf. "That hurt."

Caphy had always been over-exuberant, but she'd grown out of most of the really crazy behavior when she'd turned three. Unfortunately, adding a fun new playmate to the mix had upped the ante a bit, making her sometimes forget she wasn't a puppy anymore.

Hal grabbed a bottle of water from the fridge and handed it to me. "The lamp's still in one piece," he reported.

"Thanks," I said, taking it.

"Do you want me to make eggs or something?"

I shook my head. "I was actually thinking we should go into town for lunch."

He thought about my suggestion for a minute and then smiled. "You're going to snoop around in Arno's investigation, aren't you?"

I dropped several strawberries, some apple slices,

raw carrots, and a clump of lettuce into Ethel's bowl. "I prefer to think of it as chatting with friends."

Hal chuckled. "I'm in. I'll admit I'm not comfortable with the fact that the guy was killed at Fulle-Proof."

I settled Ethel's bowl in front of her and she dug in, happily snorfling through the food to find her favorites.

Hal handed Caphy a large, hard dog cookie. She happily retreated to her favorite spot under the kitchen table to eat it.

"Did Arno have a guess as to the time of death?" I asked as I packaged everything back up to put away.

"Yesterday sometime." Hal frowned. "Nobody's been in those buildings for months. Don't you find it strange that the day before you start packing up, a man is killed and left there?"

Closing the refrigerator door, I turned to him. "You think it's a warning?"

"I have no idea. It seems possible. We'll know more once we find out about the victim."

"Maybe you should call Cal." Cal Amity was Hal's brother. They ran a Private Investigation business in Indianapolis. Cal had lots of great contacts within local, state, and federal law enforcement.

Hal stared at me for a moment, as if there was something he wanted to say.

"What?" I asked.

"We need to consider that this could be Johnston."

Ice formed in my chest. He was right. The man still wanted my mother dead, and he was fully capable of dropping bodies as a warning or just because. "Eek!" I responded.

Hal's lips twitched. "Sorry. I knew that would freak you out. But we need to consider it."

"Have you heard anything about where he is?"

"Not a word." Hal had been keeping in touch with his friend Prudence Frect as the ongoing hunt for Edward Johnston had continued.

My mom had risked coming to Deer Hollow at Christmas, so the idea that Johnston might be in the area seemed even more terrifying.

At the look on my face, Hall pulled me into a hug. "It's going to be okay, honey. Arno knows how important it is to stay on top of this. And, whether he likes it or not, he's going to have some help." He grinned down at me and I felt better. Arno, Hal, and I had proven to be an effective team in the past.

With a lot of incentive to discover who'd killed Lucky Lucklin and hung him at my family's place of business, I knew we'd get to the bottom of the man's murder as quickly as possible.

I only hoped it was fast enough to keep my family safe.

3

Sonny's Diner was quaint. That was a good word for it. Quirky, kitschy, comfortable. All good words.

Old, tattered, and careworn were good words too. Probably a bit more accurate. But not as pleasing to the ear.

A few of those words also fit the owner of the diner, Max, who hurried toward Hal and me with two cloudy plastic glasses filled with ice water. She had a pencil tucked in the ratty nest of yellow-white hair she'd piled on top of her head.

Max chewed her gum with an energy that defied logic and tugged her order pad from an apron pocket with the slanty-eyed intensity of an Earp brother at the O.K. Corral. "Do y'all need menus?"

Hal shook his head. "I'll have a chef's salad. Oil and vinegar on the side."

Max fired lead bullets in the form of words at her order pad. "Joey?"

So efficient. Max was definitely cutting into my guilt-driven dithering time.

I chewed my lip. As always, I was torn between showing Hal my true Bumpkin side, which encompassed a lust for comfort food in the form of carbs, carbs, and more carbs; and trying to live up to his superhero eating habits. "Um..."

Hal raised his brows and said the only word that could have broken through the dam of indecision. "Meatloaf."

I groaned, nodding at Max in surrender.

Her lips twitched. "Pie?"

"Of course," Hal said. "I'll take some coffee too."

I barely kept from flinging myself at him. Hal Amity was the perfect boyfriend. He understood me and my Bumpkin appetites. And he didn't judge. He loved me despite my enormous sweet and carb tooth. Just as he adored my Pitbull despite her relentless and noisy pursuit of anything edible. And my cranky, opinionated cat, despite the fact that he was highly allergic to cats. And, of course, our adorable and equally food-driven pig.

I sipped my water, watching Max pour swamp water into a stained white mug and carry it to my PI. I grimaced as she put it down in front of him, knowing the foul-smelling sludge was going to corrupt the beautiful Greek temple from the inside out. "I don't know how you can drink that stuff," I said as she left. The water was bad enough. It tasted like it had been filtered through a rusty iron pan.

He didn't even doctor it with cream or sugar.

Sipping and grimacing slightly, Hal gave me a smile that was filled with perfect white teeth. "I need the caffeine."

The front bell jangled. I looked up to find Bobo Biddens coming through the door. He slid a small-eyed gaze over Hal and me, and then headed for the counter, where he claimed his usual red-vinyl-topped stool and ordered pie and coffee.

I hoped Max had laid our pie aside before she gave Bobo his. The thirty-something-year-old farmer and I had fought many a battle in the pie wars at Sonny's.

He must have had the same thought because, as Max placed his slice of banana cream pie in front of Bobo, he turned and gave me a crooked smile, lifting one bushy eyebrow as he forked off the creamy point of his pie.

I lifted two fingers to my eyes and then redirected them at him as he chewed. Bobo laughed, shaking his head.

Hal dropped an arm along the back of the booth and leaned in, kissing my temple. "Stop picking pie fights."

I narrowed my gaze on him. "Just making sure he knows who's in charge."

Hal chuckled. "Max put your slice aside. I saw her do it."

Relief slid through me. "Good. Then I won't need to take him down to the floor and poke him with pickle forks until he gives it over."

Max turned Bobo's mug over and filled it with sludge. "Anything else?" She asked the big man.

"I'll have the meatloaf," Bobo said, his humor-lit gaze sliding back my way.

The rat! "He ate his pie first!" I said loud enough for everyone in the diner to hear.

Bobo chuckled heartily, his fluffy body bouncing with the laughter.

Hal just shook his head.

Max, probably feeling a new episode of pie wars coming, hurried over with two slices of pie on chipped white plates. She put them down in front of us. "Here. Don't start trouble." She arched a micro-bladed light brown brow at me and turned away. "Food's up now."

I grimaced when Hal sent me a look. "I can't help myself," I said sheepishly. "I'm a pie addict."

He just shook his head again, clearly disgusted with me. But I did notice his perfect lips twitching, so maybe he was only pretending disgust.

I clung to that thought as I forked off the very tippy tip of my pie and slid the delectable treat into my mouth, nearly moaning from the buttery, creamy, sweet deliciousness of it.

We ate in companionable silence and, I was tucking the last bite of Hal's pie into my mouth when Bobo paid his bill and stood up, starting toward the door. He stopped halfway there, glancing our way. Then, frowning, the big farmer redirected toward Hal and me.

He stopped next to our table and waited silently, twisting his tattered John Deere cap in his hands. His gaze locked on mine. I gave him what I hoped was a harmless smile. "Hey," I said.

Hal stood and offered his hand. "Bobo. How are you this afternoon?"

Bobo bobbed his head in lieu of a response, still staring at me.

I tensed, wondering if he was going to call me on eating all of my pie and most of Hal's.

"Can we help you with something?" Hal asked the other man.

Bobo's dark, beady gaze finally slid away from me, landing on Hal. "My cousin's dead. I want to hire y'all to find his killer."

For just a beat, I thought Bobo was talking about a second murder. Another killer. And all the air whooshed out of my lungs as I tried to wrap my brain around my quaint little town having two killers running around in it.

But, as usual, Hal was a few beats ahead of me. "Lucky Lucklin was your cousin?"

Bobo nodded, glancing around. "Mind if I sit for a spell?"

Hal motioned toward the empty side of the booth and slid down beside me again.

We waited for Max to carry away our empties, the two men accepting "fresh" cups of swamp sludge to drink during our conversation.

Covering my empty mug, I refused the sludge Max tried to pour into it. Despite the fact that I always rejected her coffee, Max seemed determined to try to make me drink it. When she left, I settled back and sipped my iron water, wondering if it would taste better with coffee in it.

"What do you know about Lucky's death?" Hal asked Bobo.

Bobo stared at the hat he was still strangling in his big fist and frowned. As we waited for him to rub a couple of thoughts together so they'd catch fire, I noticed the probably permanent oil staining the quicks of his wide fingernails. He had hands that spoke of the hard work he did on a daily basis. Honest work. The kind that was the backbone of the country. Despite the fact that I liked to tease him, I had a deep respect for Bobo and his ilk. Farming was hard. It required a little bit of mathematics, more than a reasonable amount of engineering skill, tenaciousness in the face of adversity, and maybe just a little bit of voodoo to make it all work.

I could barely grow tomatoes in a pot on my

deck. I couldn't imagine managing several hundred acres into a bankable crop while fighting mama nature and the government's interference at every step of the way.

I'd fallen so deeply into my thoughts, I blinked in surprise when Bobo finally spoke.

Max was serving a nearby table, and Bobo seemed to be waiting for her to get out of earshot before answering Hal's question. Fortunately, the person sitting at the table was Old Man Wackerson. Deaf as a post and almost as blind.

"Lucky called me yesterday," Bobo finally said. "Early. Way too early for Luck to be awake. He sounded scared."

"Did he say what he was scared of?" Hal asked.

Bobo shook his big head. "Nah. He asked if it was okay if he stayed at my cabin out by the lakes for a few days. I told him people were renting the place at the moment, but that it would be empty in a week. That was the last I heard of him."

I thought about that, noting the holes in his story that were big enough to shove Australia through. "How do you suppose he ended up at Fulle-Proof?"

Bobo shrugged. "I've been askin' myself that too. Only thing I can think is he was hidin' there." The big man frowned. "I wish I'd known he was in trouble. I would have made him stay with me."

"Why would he be hiding?" Hal asked. "What

could your cousin have been into that got him into trouble?"

"Like I said," Bobo responded, a little angrily, "I don't know. But if I had to guess, he took somethin' that didn't belong to him. Luck had a tendency to do that. It was why he liked gamblin' so much. He liked to say he felt like he was stealin' the money he made at the tables. Probably was. I ain't never met nobody with more angles than Luck." Bobo sniffed, running a meaty finger under his nose and scraping it dry on his jeans.

"I'm sorry for your loss," I told him, belatedly.

He nodded, catching my gaze. "Honest truth, Joey, I didn't much care for old Luck. He was a scoundrel. He broke his ma's heart a few too many times for my liking. But Aunt Angie asked me to get to the bottom of it. She wants closure or some such nonsense. Ask me, she's better off makin' up her own happy endin' and just goin' with that. Any story with Lucky in it is gonna end bad. Usually, it ends poorly for everybody else. In this case, I'm afraid my cousin's own luck run out."

I reached over and patted his hand. "We'll see what we can find out."

"I'd like to speak to Lucklin's mom if you can arrange it," Hal told the farmer.

Bobo nodded and tugged a stained sheet of lined paper from his shirt pocket. The information Hal had requested was written out in a surprisingly tidy hand. He'd clearly anticipated the question.

Bobo shoved to his feet and stared down at the now-cold swamp sludge. "I'll pay whatever you charge," he said, jerking his gaze to Hal. "Just send me a bill."

Hal started to shake his head, but Bobo held up a stained and calloused hand. "No. Don't say nothin'. I pay my way. Besides, you deserve to make a livin' as much as the next guy."

Hal's mouth snapped closed, and he nodded. But I had a feeling the bill Bobo received would be a fraction of what Hal normally charged. My PI had a weakness for the people around Deer Hollow. He once told me he liked their rugged individualism. Their quiet strength. I'd never realized until he put the sentiment into words that those qualities were favorites of mine too. They were at the heart of why I stayed in the tiny country town. And the reason I'd probably never leave.

As we were sliding back into Hal's SUV, Arno called. Hal hit *Answer* on the Escalade's dash screen. "Arno."

"Hey," said the deputy. "I was wondering if you could do me a favor? Can you drop by Mitzner's and talk to him? Buck's got an abandoned car in his lot, and he's pitching a fit. I called *The Greasy Wrench* but they can't send anybody with a tow truck for a couple of hours. I thought if you took Buck's statement and got pictures of the car, it might keep him from bustin' a gut before the Wrench can get there."

Hal grinned. "Sure. We can do that." He turned at the next side street and circled around to head back out of town going North. "Bobo Biddens seems to think Lucky might have gone to the family cabin at some point."

"Okay, we'll check out the cabin. I already spoke to Angie Lucklin, but feel free to talk to her again. She might open up more to Joey than she would to me."

"Will do," Hal told Arno. "We'll stop in later to fill you in."

Buck Mitzner owned Mitzner's Landscaping north of Deer Hollow. Mitzner's was the largest business in the area and the biggest employer. The fifty-something business owner had a prickly personality that you wouldn't think would lend itself to working with customers. But somehow he made it work. Maybe because he surrounded himself with good people who helped take the edge off his temper. Though the volatile owner tended to run the weaker employees off by being a jerk on a regular basis. Unfortunately, there wasn't much of a buffer between him and them.

Hal pulled into the gravel lot and headed toward a black Lincoln Town Car parked at the back. The big car was half-hidden by several rows of deciduous saplings with newly sprouting leaves.

I glanced around the lot, mentally cataloging the goodies Buck was selling even as Spring just managed to dig her toes into the cold earth and take hold. The sun was shining, and I could almost feel cool black dirt on my hands. I was overdue to plant something in my yard.

It had been too long.

Maybe a row of flowering trees alongside my drive. That would be pretty.

Buck emerged from the office store as Hal parked the SUV.

He hurried over, a glower fixed on his face. It looked perfectly natural on him.

"People think that just because I have a business along the highway, they have the right to just dump their Rent-a-Wrecks in my lot. I'm sick of it."

I eyed the expensive black sedan and lifted a brow. "Rent-a-Wreck?"

Buck's lips curled. "You know what I mean. Arno needs to come get this piece of crap out of my lot, or I'm gonna bulldoze it into the back and plant trees in the frame."

Buck was in rare form. I tried to remember that he was dealing with something which probably contributed to his volatile personality. Reverend Smythe of the Lutheran church downtown had told me Buck's secret not all that long ago. Well, he hadn't exactly told me. He'd more insinuated it. But I got the gist.

Buck was fighting substance abuse. And it seemed his battles were hard-won. At the expense of his better nature.

"When did this show up here?" Hal asked, ignoring Buck's bluster.

"How do I know? I was asleep."

Hal lowered his sunglasses and peered over them until Buck seemed to rethink his hostile attitude. He scrubbed a hand wearily over his eyes. "I left at nine last night, and it was here when I arrived at six this morning."

Hal nodded. "Has anything been disturbed?"

Buck blinked. He'd apparently been so annoyed by the arrival of the car he hadn't thought about what it might mean. "I...we haven't really looked."

Hal inclined his head. "Can you have someone do a quick inventory of the place, please? Let's make sure this is just a dumped car and not something worse."

I fought a smile as Buck turned on his heel and rushed back the way he'd come. "Nice work. That should keep him busy until the tow truck gets here."

Hal didn't respond. I glanced at his face and noted the frown there. My antennas immediately went up. "What's wrong?"

Hal crouched down by the back bumper of the shiny car, pointing to the chrome latch there. "Unless I'm in a pie coma and dreaming, I'm pretty sure that right there is a bloody fingerprint."

4

Hal and I stood back and watched as Arno and his people got the trunk open and looked inside. Arno turned to us and shook his head, and Hal expelled a long breath. "No body."

He didn't sound relieved, however, which made me wonder what he'd been thinking.

Arno came over and nodded toward Mitzner's office. "You spoke to Buck?"

"More like got yelled at by him," I told my friend the deputy. "He's just mad somebody dumped a car here. He hadn't even considered why somebody might have done that."

"I asked him to do an inventory to see if anything was disturbed." Hal frowned. "Then I saw the blood."

Arno nodded. "We'll search the area for the body

that isn't in that trunk. I'll be surprised if we find it here, though."

"Is it possible that blood belonged to Lucky Lucklin?" Hal asked.

"Could be," Arno said, staring at the abandoned car. "But it seems unlikely. As far as I could see, the only wound Lucklin had was the one that killed him, and he bled out where we found him."

"So we're looking for a second corpse," I said, frowning. "What in the world is going on?"

"That's what we need to find out," Arno said with a bit too much attitude for my taste.

I narrowed my gaze at him. "Have you heard from Lis?"

Arno's handsome face turned pink. He slid his gaze toward his boots, clearly made uncomfortable by my question.

It was probably mean of me to bring my best friend Lis Villa up to Arno. The two of them had been dancing around a relationship for years, with very limited success. They'd recently seemed to have made progress in that direction, even going so far as to have a movie night together the last time Lis had been home. But something had happened that neither of them would tell me about, and their budding romance seemed to have taken another hit.

I thought maybe Arno was being cranky with me because of Lis. He probably assumed Lis had told me why she'd left Deer Hollow again and hadn't been back for weeks. But she hadn't told me anything. And she'd made it pretty clear she wouldn't. So I'd be danged if I was going to let Arno punish me for whatever it was he'd done wrong.

"No. She's been too busy to return my calls." He lifted his head, fixing me with an intense brown gaze. "Have you?"

"Not a peep."

He stared at me for a long moment, as if trying to judge if I was telling him the truth. I held his gaze, nothing to hide. Finally, he nodded. "We'll send a sample of the blood to the lab and see if it's a match for Lucklin. But I'm not hopeful."

"For all we know they could have hit a deer and thrown it into the trunk," Hal suggested.

Arno nodded. "Could be."

"Deputy Willager!"

We all turned at the sound of Buck Mitzner's voice. He was standing near the back of the deciduous tree lot, looking anxious.

Arno hurried in that direction and Hal and I fell in behind him. I stayed as quiet as a little mouse in the hopes he wouldn't notice me and send me away. Hal was a former cop and a current Private Investigator. He had the background to serve as a fill-in deputy for the Sheriff's Department.

I was just his nosy girlfriend. Which usually placed me on the razor edge of being sent away when stuff got interesting.

Buck was wringing his hands, his face flushed and coated with an amount of sweat that seemed excessive given the sixty-degree temps. "I didn't touch anything, I promise. I was just looking for missing trees when I found it."

Hal and I stopped several feet away from a disturbed area between the burlap-tied root balls of two small trees. The mulch that had been nestled around the roots had been pulled away and was spread over the nearby grass, a small tree flung on its side a few feet away from the spot.

A shovel lay nearby, rich black dirt coating its blade.

Arno nodded toward the tree on the grass. "I take it that's out of place?"

Buck nodded. "And that's one of our shovels, but my people wouldn't leave it out here in the elements. I'd tan their hides for it."

Arno walked around the hole, taking care not to touch anything or step into the soft dirt near the freshly-dug hole. Hal walked over and crouched next to the shovel, examining it as well as he could without touching it. "Arno." He pointed to a dark smear on the implement's handle. "Does that look like blood to you?"

Arno crouched next to him and sighed, shaking his head. He straightened alongside Hal and the two men each took a large step backward, away from the shovel. Arno pulled his cell out of a pocket and dialed. "Sheppard, I need you and a crime scene tech out to Mitzner's ASAP."

When he disconnected, he looked at Buck, an apologetic expression on his face. "I'm afraid we're going to have to do some digging here, Mr. Mitzner. We're going to make a mess. It can't be avoided."

Mitzner's usual glower deepened. "Is that really necessary?"

"I'm afraid so. Whoever dumped that car here was carrying something that bled in its trunk. And they also seemed to have done some digging here. There's a better than fifty percent chance he or she buried something in this spot."

Mitzner crossed beefy arms over his chest, looking murderous. "I'll be sending a bill to the Sheriff's Department."

Arno shrugged. I got the impression he was happy not to be the one to have to deal with that end of things. There were advantages to not being the boss. "You do what you need to do, Mr. Mitzner."

The owner whipped angrily around, stomping toward the office as he pulled a cell phone from his pocket.

I looked at Arno. "He's calling the Sheriff to tattle on you."

Arno snorted. "Yeah."

"Will Sheriff Mulhern back you up?" Hal asked.

Arno didn't hesitate. "Yes. Since it's just Mitzner.

If it was a politician with any power at all, I'd be toast."

I would have laughed but realized it wasn't really funny. Politicians were pretty much all scum.

"Have your people run the car yet?" Hal asked Arno.

"Oh, yeah, Sheppard ran it. I meant to tell you. There's no obvious connection to Lucklin. It belongs to a man in Indianapolis. He reported it stolen last night. Nothing to help us there."

"Except that the killers probably came from Indianapolis," I said.

Arno frowned but nodded. "It looks that way. If..." He eyed me carefully. "Don't assume this has anything to do with your mom, Joey. We don't have any evidence of that at this point. For all we know, that blood is Lucklin's." He nodded toward the shovel.

I didn't respond because I couldn't help feeling that speaking the fear out loud would make it too real. The last time we'd had bodies dropping all over Deer Hollow, it had had everything to do with my mom. And the connection to Indianapolis was more than concerning.

Hal grabbed my hand. "We're going to talk to Lucklin's mom and anybody else he might have been in contact with. We'll touch base later?"

Arno nodded. "You know his mom?"

Hal slid me a glance. "No. But her nephew visited us at lunch."

Arno's eyebrows rose and he glanced at me.

"Bobo Biddens," I reminded him. "He wanted to hire us to find Lucky's killer."

Arno thought about that. "Okay. Run your parallel investigation. Just let me know if you discover anything that will help me with this one."

Hal nodded. "We'll keep you informed."

As we headed back to Hal's Escalade, a white van bearing the insignia of the Crime Scene Unit from Nashville, Indiana pulled in, parking behind the abandoned car from Indy.

I frowned. "Do you think that's Lucky's blood?" I asked Hal, buckling myself in.

His gaze slid toward the tree lot where we'd left Arno. "I don't know. That blood smear on the shovel is bothering me."

"You think Arno's gonna uncover another body?"

Hal's handsome face was taut with concern. "I think that's a distinct possibility."

"Maybe Lucky took something from somebody and buried it there."

"Could be. We'll know soon enough." He pulled out the note from Bobo, handing it to me. "You know where this is?"

I did. "Head South on Highway 65. It's about five miles out of town."

Angie Lucklin lived off a dusty gravel road that fed a smattering of farmhouses and a few much newer and much nicer homes arrayed on large parcels of land. It was mostly farmland, flat and uninspiring, but there were enough spurts of trees scattered around the homes and along the road to make it pretty.

I couldn't see it in the distance, but I knew the Fawn River wound its way along behind the homes on Angie Lucklin's side of the road.

The leaves had emerged on the trees around Deer Hollow a couple of weeks earlier and the vibrant green of new growth sparkled in the late afternoon light.

The fog from that morning was a distant memory, burned off by a determined sunlight that had heated the temps to a pleasant mid-sixties. Early flowers poked from the ground in kidney-shaped flower beds decorating the newer homes and nestled beneath mailboxes in the older ones.

I lowered my window and inhaled deeply, enjoying the fresh scent of the flowers and grass and the distant tang of manure that was so much a part of Deer Hollow.

"I love Spring."

Hal nodded, his gaze sliding over the mailboxes in search of the house where Angie lived. He slowed when he saw the number 10694 on a fish-shaped mailbox that was beyond ugly. I smiled at the trout's wide mouth that served as the mailbox opening, the weird container appealing to my quirky design sense.

"That's an odd mailbox for a landlocked farm," Hal said.

"The Fawn is nearby. It's a popular fishing spot in Deer Hollow."

He nodded, conceding the point.

We followed a quarter-mile-long gravel drive toward a small clapboard home that was painted a soft yellow. White shutters framed the front windows and the long front porch was flamboyant with large pots of flowers.

The place was slightly worn but pretty, with a backdrop of woods that wrapped around it to provide a living green frame.

A tall woman stepped from the house as Hal parked in front of a detached, two-car garage.

He'd called Angie on the way and she'd seemed eager to talk to us.

She stood on the porch, her narrow face pinched and worn and her hands sliding over her arms as if trying to ward off the cold.

Lucky Lucklin's mom was dressed in black yoga pants and a plain gray tee-shirt with a vee-neck. Her feet were bare against the well-worn boards of the covered porch. Angie's graying blonde hair was pulled back into a tight bun at the back of her head, a few frizzy strands framing her round cheeks.

She moved forward as we approached, her expression tired and sad. "Hello." Angie Lucklin offered her hand to me and I took it, giving it a squeeze. "I'm Joey Fulle, Mrs. Lucklin. This is Hal Amity. We were hoping to speak to you about Luck... um...Lance."

"Please, call me Angie." She gave us a weary smile. The sun slid over her face, highlighting its ashen hue and the soft lines at the corners of her eyes and mouth. "Bobo told me you'd be coming by. I was glad when you called. I needed to talk to someone. What happened to my boy isn't right. Someone needs to look into it." She stared into my eyes. "Someone who'll consider *his* side of things."

I nodded, not knowing what else to do. "Hal and I will examine the evidence with open minds," I told her. "I can make that promise to you."

Angie held my gaze a moment longer, clearly looking for hidden meanings behind my words, and then nodded. "Come inside. I have coffee."

Hal's phone rang and he looked at the ID. "I need to take this," he told me.

I nodded, realizing he meant in private. I glanced at Angie. "He'll be in shortly."

Angie watched Hal trot down the steps and walk back to the car as he answered the phone, a speculative gleam in her pale brown gaze. She opened her mouth, and the words that fell out weren't at all what I expected. "He's a fine-looking man."

I blinked in surprise. It wasn't that I was surprised she'd noticed. Women always noticed Hal. Especially after they'd spent a few minutes in his company. His quiet strength, unassuming competence, and innate kindness only strengthened his appeal. I constantly wrestled with the jealously that lived inside. I still wasn't sure what he saw in me. I wasn't confident that he'd keep seeing it if we stayed together for very long.

None of that was new.

But Angie Lucklin had just lost her son. I was a little surprised she had it in her to notice a good-looking man at that point in her life.

At a loss for an adequate response, I simply nodded.

When she realized I wasn't going to spill my guts about Hal and my relationship, Angie jerked her head toward the screen door. "Let's get inside, out of this heat."

Like Hal's appeal to other women, the heat wasn't a surprise. But it *was* unusual for so early in Spring. What had been temps in the sixties just an hour earlier was beginning to feel like mid-seventies in the bright sun. It was nice. But I kept expecting Old Man Winter to scream, "Just kidding!" and fling some more snow at us. So, at that moment, I was fully embracing the heat. The brutal cold was too close in my memory to do otherwise. I nodded, wanting to give Hal some privacy for his call.

I followed the other woman past a careworn but comfortable-looking living room at the front of the house and into a careworn and comfortable-looking kitchen at the back. Something about Angie Lucklin was tugging at my memories. "Have we met before?" I finally asked. "You seem so familiar."

Angie smiled. "We might have. I used to teach at the high school."

That's what it was. "Math?"

She nodded, her smile widening. "And economics. I'm surprised you remembered me. I only worked there for a couple of years."

"It's probably because those were two of my least favorite subjects," I admitted sheepishly.

She laughed as she pulled mugs from a cabinet.

I looked around the kitchen.

The black and white squares of linoleum could have been new, retro, but I suspected they were the real thing. Along with the "real" Formica counter-tops and "genuine" butcher block island at the center of the small space.

I sat down at a round table, the top not heavy enough to be genuine or expensive. But the vinyl cushioned chairs were comfortable, and the table was cute. At its center, a glass vase of assorted flowers perfumed the air with their soft fragrance and gave the room a cheery focal point.

Angie poured coffee into two mugs and set them on the table. "Cream?"

I nodded. "Please."

By the time Angie was sitting at the table with me, Hal had come inside, his gaze briefly sliding to mine before returning to Angie. "This is a nice place," he told her with a smile that made the ligaments in my knees melt.

From the way she coughed out a nervous laugh, I figured Angie wasn't unaffected. "It isn't much, but it's home. Things have gotten a bit run down since Mr. Lucklin passed."

"When did you lose him?" I asked, hoping small-talk would ease the woman's nerves about having us there.

"Two years ago," Angie said. "I can't believe he's been gone that long." She smiled. "He was a cop in Ormsville."

"How'd he die?" Unlike me, Hal seemed more than casually interested.

"Ruptured aneurism, exacerbated by anti-coagulant meds." She shook her head. "Ironic that the drug meant to keep him healthy ended up killing him."

Hal sipped his black coffee. "I'm sorry for your loss."

Angie stared at her untouched coffee for a long moment and then said. "I know Lance wasn't a perfect human being. But he wasn't a bad person. It's possible he made some regrettable decisions. But whatever he did, he didn't deserve to be killed like that."

Moisture pooled in her gaze and slid unnoticed down her pale cheeks. "I hope you'll find the person who did this to him."

"We're certainly going to try," Hal told her gently. "Actually, you can help."

Angie's head snapped up. "Me? How?"

"We need to look into everybody he knew in the area. All his connections. If he worked with anybody who was in any way questionable, we need to know that too."

"Anything you can tell us might help," I said.

Angie shrugged. "I haven't kept up with his friends the last year or two. He hasn't been around much."

Hal leaned across the table. "What kind of car did Lance drive?"

Angie sipped thoughtfully. "Last time he was here, he was driving a beater. She shook her head. I don't know much about cars. All I know is it was boxy and rusting."

"Do you remember the color?"

"Pinkish brown." She wrinkled her nose. "I remember because I thought it was a strange color for a man."

"Phone number?" Hal asked. "Address. Frequent hangouts. Place of business."

"I can give you his phone number. I don't know if the address he gave me is still current, but you're welcome to it." She frowned. "When he lived here in Deer Hollow, he hung out with the Burrows boys." She glanced at me. "You know the Burrows?"

Unfortunately, I did. Trouble. Every last one of them. They didn't live in Deer Hollow but they spent a lot of time here anyway. I nodded, glancing at Hal. "Ten kids. Nine of them boys. The one daughter moved away at eighteen. Put herself through college and never came back. The last I heard, she was using her mother's maiden name and she'd become a doctor."

Hal sipped, listening.

"All but one of the boys was trouble," Angie said. "Three of 'em ended up in prisons around the country. Two of them were in Juvie before they turned thirteen. The ones who haven't been in jail haven't made anything of themselves. They spend their time trying to rip people off. I told Lance to stay away from those boys. Of course, he never listened."

"Was there one in particular who he hung out with?" I asked.

"George." Angie grimaced at the name as if she'd bitten down on something foul. "They used to hang out all the time until George ran his motorcycle into the side of my minivan a few years back and banged himself up pretty badly. He tried to sue me for the damages, but the cop who came to the scene was a friend of mine from the academy. He ran a breatha-lyzer on that little thug, and George was sitting at twice the legal limit."

"You went to the academy?" Hal asked, smiling.

She laughed. "Yes. Twelve years ago. I was a bored housewife and wanted to do something useful. I barely passed the physical stuff. But I was a pretty good marksman. My papa taught all of us girls to shoot when we were barely out of diapers."

"Like *The Rookie*?" I asked, grinning. The television show about the middle-aged man who became a cop was one of my favorites.

She laughed again, nodding. "Except he managed to pass. I was an academy dropout."

Still, it was an interesting factoid that I hadn't known. And it just went to show. You should never judge people until you got to know them.

Everybody has their little secrets.

5

Hal was quiet as we drove away from Angie Lucklin's home. Thoughtful.

I left him to his thoughts for several moments, lost in my own musings.

"Pru called," he finally said, turning to look at me as I sent him a surprised glance. "She had news about our case," he added.

I felt my eyes growing wide. "You consulted her about it?" I fought a spear of jealousy. Pru was about as close to perfect as a person could get. And she'd known Hal a lot longer than I had. I knew it was stupid to be jealous. Hal hadn't shown any interest in her at all. But I didn't seem able to help myself.

Hal shook his head. "No. It never occurred to me. But she talked to Arno about a case she's been working in Indy. He told her to call me."

Relief slipped through me. "What case?"

"There's been a series of armored car robberies. The crew is fast, professional, and seems to have inside information. Targets are varied enough that the informant isn't likely to be attached to any of the locations where the heists occurred."

I thought about what he was telling me, my mind struggling to find the connection to Lucky Lucklin's death. "Did Lucky work for the armored car company?"

Hal shook his head. "No. Or any of the targets."

"Then, what's the connection?"

Hal turned into my driveway and accelerated toward the house. "There might not be one. But the last robbery, outside of a casino in French Lick, Indiana, was interrupted."

"The police?"

Hal parked in the circular drive before the house, cutting the engine and staring straight ahead for a moment. "According to Pru, someone stumbled into the robbery. Someone who was either very lucky or not lucky at all."

"Lucky? That's a familiar theme."

He gave me a sad smile. "A drunk driver rammed the armored car while the thieves were removing the bags of money. One of the thieves was killed. The other was thrown from the scene and was unconscious." He turned to me. "Security cameras at the back of the casino caught the accident. They also caught the driver, clearly drunk out of his mind, stumbling out of his car, looking over the downed thieves, and then finding the money."

"Was it Lucky?"

Hal shrugged. "He was wearing a cap and either knew where the cameras were or just got…"

"Lucky," I said, nodding. I thought about it. "I'm guessing he took the money?"

"He did. And drove away in a very battered sedan. Tan with four doors. The accident destroyed the grill, and when the man backed away he smacked into a tree. The crash bent the back bumper and the plate so badly the camera couldn't capture it."

"He was *really* lucky," I breathed, shaking my head.

"Yeah."

"So why did Pru call Arno?"

"She's calling all the law enforcement in the area to find out if anybody local showed up in a battered tan sedan and suddenly seemed to have a lot of money."

"That makes sense." I thought about it for another minute, then glanced at Hal. "That's why you asked Angie what kind of car Lucky drove?" He'd been trying to tie Lucklin to the abandoned car from Indy.

Hal nodded. "It was a stretch, but worth a shot."

"Angie said pinkish brown. I've seen pinkish-brown cars before. They're kind of tan."

Hal nodded. "He could have stolen the Town Car if he thought his car had been compromised. It seems unlikely, if he was as drunk as Pru described. But it's possible."

Hal nodded. "Crime Scene should be able to find fingerprints or other DNA in the car if Lucklin drove it."

"Not to mention blood."

"Yeah. But the blood wouldn't necessarily mean he was driving."

I thought about the blood in the trunk and realized Lucky could have just as easily traveled to Deer Hollow in the trunk of that car. "Yeah. You're right."

Hal climbed out and came around the car, opening my door for me and offering me his hand. I let him help me out because I loved that his instincts led him to do it. And, because I was a klutz and therefore just as likely to fall on my face climbing down from the big car as I was to descend agilely from it.

Hal dropped an arm around my shoulders, and we moved companionably toward the front door. Pibl warbling and barking greeted us from inside the home. A beat later, a wild-eyed Pitbull bounced off the window in the living room and pattered noisily to the front door to bounce impatiently on the tile.

"One of these days, she's going to go right through that glass," Hal said, frowning worriedly.

"I know. I'm tempted to board it up, so she

doesn't hurt herself." I hated to admit how close I'd come to it. But both Caphy and LaLee loved to look out that window during the day when I was gone. I was reluctant to take their fun away from them. Not to mention it would look really ugly.

"We could replace it with plexiglass," Hal suggested as if he'd read my mind. "That way, they can still see out."

I loved that idea. To let him know, I touched his lips in a gentle kiss, letting him pull me close and deepen the kiss as a reward for being so thoughtful.

Okay, I might have been rewarding myself too.

After a moment, the sound of a pibl flinging herself at the door was too much for us. I broke the kiss on a sigh.

"She's spoiled rotten," Hal said, arching a midnight brow accusingly at me.

I gave him a crooked smile. "And your point is?"

He snorted, using his key to open the door.

"Besides," I told him as the pibl flew through the door, swiped a wet tongue over my hand and Hal's knee, and then took off into the yard. "You spoil her every bit as much as I do."

Hal didn't argue, probably because it was true. "I'm going to call Arno and fill him in."

I nodded. "Beer?"

"Please."

"I guess we need to go talk to George Burrows?" I said later, as we ate dinner.

Hal stabbed a bite of baked potato and nodded. "It seems logical. Though I can't shake the feeling that the murder is somehow tied to Pru's case."

I nodded, offering a small bite of my steak to Caphy under the table. Never one to be left out, LaLee put her paws, claws out in silent threat, on my leg. I gave her a bite too, then glanced toward the snorfling noises coming from the tent in the corner of the kitchen. I smiled. I'd give Ethel Squeaks the rest of my baked potato when she finished her snack of strawberries and raw veggies. "So maybe we need to take a trip to French Lick," I told him, waggling my brows.

French Lick, Indiana was a gorgeous area in the southern part of the state, nearly to Kentucky. I loved visiting the wineries there and had always wanted to go spelunking in the area's caves.

Hal snorted. "That would be a shame."

The doorbell rang, and Caphy tore toward the front of the house. Her tail whipped the air as she barked with delighted anticipation. I stood as a voice called out.

"Joey? Hal? You here?"

"In the kitchen." I went to the kitchen door and looked toward the front entrance, where Arno was currently crouched down fending off Caphy's agile tongue. He gave LaLee a scratch behind the ears as she wound through his legs, yowling at him for not being there sooner to act as her human servant. With his free hand, he threw Ethel's favorite yellow ball into the living room so she could chase it.

I laughed. "I never knew you were such a multi-tasker."

Arno shook his head, straightening. "I'm a man of many talents." His expression turned serious. "I was wondering if I could ask you a few questions?"

"Sure. Are you off duty? Would you like a beer?"

"That would be great. Thanks."

Hal stood as Arno came into the kitchen, shaking his hand. "Did you have any luck at Mitzner's?"

He shook his head. "My men are still looking. The place is huge. He has no fewer than fifteen outbuildings on a hundred acres." Arno took the bottle of beer from me. "Thanks, Joey."

I motioned toward the extra chair at the table as Hal cleared the plates.

"I hope I didn't interrupt your dinner?" Arno said, frowning.

"Nope. We were done," Hal told him. "Caphy will be mad though, she was about to get the rest of Joey's steak."

I arched my brows. "Don't think I didn't see you sneaking her your broccoli."

Arno grimaced. "She eats broccoli? Yuck. I thought she was smarter than that."

I laughed. "Caphy will eat anything that won't eat her back."

"Do you have news?" Hal asked.

Arno skimmed me a look that made my pulse flutter with alarm. "Is it about the auction?"

"I'm afraid so. The crime scene techs found evidence that Lucky Lucklin had been living there."

My eyes went wide. "Living there? Where?"

"In the office. They found a sleeping bag and some supplies in one of the owner offices."

I glanced at Hal. "We were in the building this morning."

"Which office?" Arno was frowning, "Did you touch anything?"

"We only packed up the outer office," Hal told him.

I nodded in agreement. "I was going to get to the other offices this afternoon." I slumped in my chair. "You know why that never happened."

"I have your fingerprints on file. We'll make sure to exclude your prints from the record."

I didn't respond. I was suddenly so tired. Depressed. A task that had been difficult to start had turned impossible and devastating. And I hadn't even had time for it to really sink in. I suddenly wished I could talk to my mom about everything. The auction was more hers than mine. She had a right to know what was going on. At the end of that same thought, I realized I wouldn't want to scare her with the knowledge I was currently trying to come to grips with.

"Joey, I have to ask about keys." Arno's handsome face was tight. He didn't look happy.

I blinked. "Keys? What keys?"

"Lance Lucklin had a key to your property. How do you suppose he got hold of that key?"

Arno stared at me for a long moment while I tried to wrap my mind around his question. Did he believe I'd had something to do with Lucky's murder? "What exactly are you asking me, Arno?"

His jaw tightened. "It's not a trick question, Joey. I'm not trying to trip you up. We found a key for your property with Lucklin's belongings. There are no signs that he broke into the auction property. No breached fencing, no broken locks. He clearly used the key to get inside. I need to know how he got the key. It could be important."

I shook my head, staring at my empty bottle of beer. "He didn't get the key from me. I have no idea how he would have gotten it." I thought about what Arno was asking me. Had I been careless with the keys? I didn't believe I had. I hadn't hidden them away. "I keep my keys hanging on those hooks over there by the door. In the mudroom."

Arno walked over and eyed the keys in question, taking in the immediate area. "These keys are close to the door. Someone could just break the window and reach inside for them."

I tried to keep my expression neutral. That had never occurred to me. I was suffering under the challenge of not being a criminal and therefore not thinking like one, as well as having country-itis. Country people don't generally worry about locks and security. It just doesn't seem important. At least not until they've suffered from the laxity.

"Nobody's broken into the house since..." I frowned. The last time had been when I'd learned my mom was still alive. A crazy killer had nearly murdered Hal and me that time. I'd been a lot more security conscious after that.

"Joey's careful, Arno," Hal said, placing a big, warm hand on my back in support. He'd no doubt seen the haunted look on my face that memories of that time inspired. "You don't believe she had something to do with this, do you?"

I winced. I hadn't wanted to come right out and ask, probably because I was afraid of Arno's response.

"I have no reason to think that," Arno said, his brown gaze neutral. "I'm just running down details."

Hal nodded, his hand rubbing gentle circles between my shoulder blades.

A cacophony of clacking sounds headed toward us from the living room, where the pibl and the pig had been playing with Ethel Squeaks' yellow ball together.

Dog and pig skidded into the room, Caphy slamming up against the island cabinets in lieu of brakes and Ethel snorfling happily over to Arno. Never one to be shy with visitors, she eagerly bumped him with her snout.

He smiled, reaching down to scratch the little pig between her oversized ears. "Hey, girl. You're looking good." He glanced up at Hal. "You're taking good care of her. Have you given any more thought to letting my mom have her?"

Hal and I shared a look and he grinned. "I don't think so, Arno. But thanks. Joey and I consider her part of the family."

I looked at my silly Pitbull and smiled as she nosed the ball toward Ethel, eager to continue their play. "Caphy would be devastated if she left."

Watching me, Arno said, "Mm-hm. *Caphy* would be devastated."

My vision blurred under embarrassed tears. "Hal would miss her a lot too."

Arno straightened to his full height, scratching his dense, blond hair and pursing his perfect lips. "Do you know what's going on with Lis?"

I almost sighed. I really wished my two friends could get their acts together. They'd been dancing around a relationship since high school and neither one could seem to find a way around their natural resistance to make it work. I shook my head. "I ran into her mom last week, and she said Lis was doing some freelance work in Indy."

Melissa Villa, though everybody called her Lis, had been my best friend since grade school. She currently lived in Indianapolis and had been a fashion model until problems had arisen with her agency. They'd taken advantage of a teen's short-sightedness in encouraging her to sign a bad contract just out of high school without her parents' knowledge. The agency had treated Lis like an indentured servant and had recently dropped her altogether. I wasn't sure what Lis was currently doing. But I was anxious to see her and find out. "Mrs. Villa thought Lis would be home for a visit in the next couple of weeks."

Arno's expression turned briefly hopeful before he brutally squelched it. "I should get going. If you think of anything on that key, will you let me know?"

I nodded, thoughtfully.

Hal walked him to the front door. The two men stood outside on the porch for a few minutes talking. I busied myself cleaning up the dishes, looking up when Hal came inside. I glanced at him as he came into the kitchen. "Do you think he'll ever admit he loves her?"

Hal blinked in surprise. His mind had obviously been on other things. "Arno and Lis?"

I nodded, drying my hands on a towel.

"Eventually. If she'll stay put long enough for him to work up the courage."

I chuckled. There was that. Lis had always been antsy. Even when we were kids, she'd had grand ideas about seeing the world. She'd done a lot of traveling as a fashion model, and I got the impression that the experience had dulled some of her appetite to flit around. But I wasn't sure it was enough to get her to settle down.

"Arno wants us to talk to George Burrows," Hal said.

I nodded, stuffing the towel through a drawer pull near the sink. "I'm ready when you are."

6

A muddy but muscular motorcycle sat in the narrow front yard of the duplex where George Burrows lived. The grass was long, the bushes untrimmed, and empty beer cans lined the warped and pitted wood railing of the small porch.

The aluminum screen door was covered in dents. The lower screen had come loose from the frame, blowing gently in a soft, cool breeze. The interior door was open, allowing us to peer down a short hallway and through a shabbily appointed living space to a smeared and cloudy sliding door in the back wall.

The other half of the duplex was tidy to the point of OCD. I couldn't help wondering how the person living next to George Burrows was enjoying his ownership style. The spicy-sweet scent of barbeque met us at the door.

My nose twitched with pleasure at the delicious smell.

Hal knocked on the screen door and we waited, looking down the short street filled with similar duplex homes. Like the duplex where Burrows lived, there was a mix of well-kept and country-cluttered. There was even an old sports car on blocks in the driveway three duplexes down from where we stood.

Hal knocked again, louder and longer.

The door to the adjoining duplex opened. A small woman with a puffy brown pageboy and slightly pinched features peered out at us. Despite her resting bitter face, the woman's tone was calm and kind as she spoke. "He's in back, barbequing his dinner."

I gave her a smile, and Hal reached across the narrow space between the porches, taking care not to step into a tiny flower bed filled with plump red geraniums. I was pretty sure George hadn't planted them.

"Thank you," Hal said, taking her slim hand in a gentle grip. "I'm Hal Amity and this is Joey Fulle."

The woman skimmed me a quick look and then returned her gaze to Hal. Though nothing in her expression changed, I got the distinct impression she was admiring the view. "Patti Lou Fredricks. It's a pleasure." She pointed toward Burrows' half of the building. "There's a space between the buildings down there that you can use to get around back."

"I appreciate that," Hal said. "I wonder if you'd mind answering a couple of questions?"

The woman's RBF pinched a little tighter, but she nodded. "What's this about?"

"We're helping Deputy Willager with an investigation," Hal said. He showed her the picture of Lance Lucklin Angie had given us. "Do you recognize this man?"

Patti Lou gave the photo a careful look and then shook her head. "Never seen him before. Should I have?"

"He's a good friend of Mr. Burrows," I told her. "We were hoping you might have seen him around here."

"Did something happen to him?" Something in the way she asked made me wonder if she was lying about not knowing him.

"He was killed."

The woman blinked rapidly, her pinched lips opening in surprise. "Oh. Well, that's terrible."

"Yes," Hal said. He didn't say anything more, no doubt hoping she'd fill the silence with the information she wasn't giving us.

"Well," Patti Lou finally said. "I need to get back inside."

"You said we could get around back going this way?" Hal said, giving her the smile that melted knee ligaments.

Patti Lou swallowed hard, her non-descript blue

eyes going wide. "Yes."

"I wonder, did you happen to notice if Mr. Burrows was home last night?"

"Oh, I wouldn't know. I'm not nosy like that."

And my name is Petunia Lickerbacher, I thought.

"Of course you aren't," Hal readily agreed.

I barely kept from snorting. I didn't know how he did that. How he pretended to believe people who were obviously lying. He was really good at it.

"But, I thought maybe you heard his bike." Hal grinned. "I know how loud these things can be."

Patti Lou succumbed to his charm, smiling back. "It is loud. And to tell you the truth, I'm a light sleeper. I heard him leave around seven last night, and his bike woke me up around eleven."

Hal nodded. "That's very helpful, Patti. Thank you so much."

Patti flushed with pleasure, skimming me a speculative look. She stepped forward, her hands resting on the post support for the metal roof of her porch. "I wonder, would you like to come inside..." She flushed. "For something hot."

Oh no she didn't! I coughed into my hand and turned away. The woman probably hadn't meant that the way it sounded.

Right.

"Thank you, Patti Lou. We need to speak to Mr. Burrows. But I really appreciate your help."

Too embarrassed for Patti Lou to look at her. I

walked around George's motorcycle, examining the wide tires and noticing the gravel stuck between the tread. My gaze slid toward the road at the end of the drive and I frowned.

"What do you see?" Hal asked.

I pointed to the white chunks of stone stuck in Burrows' tires. It looked a lot like the gravel at the auction lot. "The roads out here are all paved." I pointed to the cracked concrete drive. "Where do you suppose he picked up this gravel?"

Hal pulled a small knife from his pocket and opened it with a snap of his wrist. He extracted a clean handkerchief from the other pocket and, using the knife to carefully dig some of the stones from the bike's tires, he wrapped them in the hanky and replaced it in his pocket. "Maybe Arno's CSU techs can figure out where it came from."

I nodded as the door opened and a big, burly guy came out onto the porch.

"What are you doing to my bike?"

Burrow's face was dark with rage, his posture stiff with it. He came down the steps at an aggressive rate of speed, his big hands clenched into fists.

Hal stepped in front of me, holding up his hands, palms out. "George Burrows?"

Burrows jerked to a stop, his dark, hostile gaze sliding over Hal and back to his bike. "What were you doing to my tires?"

Hal pointed to the chunks of gravel embedded

there. "We were wondering where that gravel came from."

Burrows scowled belligerently at Hal. My PI was almost a foot taller than the other man. No wonder Barrows had skidded to a stop. "None of your business. Who are you? What are you doing here?"

I decided a softer touch might get us a bit further. I smiled at Burrows. "Hey, George," I said. "I'm Joey Fulle. I think we have some of the same friends."

His lips curled as he looked at me. "I doubt it, sugar. I'm pretty sure you and I have never met."

I forced my smile to stay curved across my tight face. "No. We haven't met. But I knew your friend, Lance Lucklin."

Burrows' broad, ruddy face lost a tiny bit of its hostility. "Lucky? What about him? I haven't seen him in days."

"Lucky Lucklin's dead," Hal told the other man. "Murdered."

Burrows stared at me for a long beat and then glanced away. I wasn't sure how to interpret that stare, but it made me uncomfortable. He shook his head. "I had no idea." He crossed his arms over his tee-shirt-clad chest and then seemed to suffer a jolt of understanding. His gaze jerked back to Hal's. "You think I killed him?"

"Is there a reason we should think that?" Hal asked.

Burrows bristled again, his knuckles cracking as he clenched them tighter.

I frowned, wondering why Hal kept poking the bear. He usually had a lighter touch.

"I have no idea!" Burrows screamed, getting into Hal's face. "Unless you're gonna arrest me, you need to get off my property, or I'm callin' the cops." He hesitated, his brows lowering over the angry brown gaze. "You aren't cops." He sneered at me. "What are you, reporters?"

Biting back indignation, I stepped up next to Hal. "Now, that's just insulting."

Burrows snorted out a laugh.

"We spoke to Angie Lucklin, and she told us you and Lance were good friends," Hal said, leaning closer to me. I almost sighed. I was glad that he was protective, but I doubted George Burrows was going to punch me with Hal mere inches away.

George shrugged. "We've been friends for a long time. Lucky was actually closer to my younger brother Pim. They got into trouble together a lot in school."

"I don't remember Pim," I told Burrows, frowning.

"His name's Robbie, but he always had pimples growin' up. Everybody called him Pimple, but it eventually got shortened to Pim." George picked at a sliver of flaking paint on the door frame. "Pim and

Lance." He laughed. "I used to tease 'em that they sounded like a bad sitcom."

"Do you think your brother kept in touch?" Hal asked.

"Nah. Pim moved to Indianapolis a year or so ago. Like my sister, he managed to escape bumpkinville, and he never looked back. Last I heard, he was making decent scratch working for some rich guy."

"Why'd he leave?" I asked.

Burrows shrugged. "He and my dad didn't see eye to eye on things. Not that that was unusual. My dad's kind of a di..."

"You don't believe they still hung out?" Hal interrupted.

"I don't know. Pim and Lucky hadn't been getting' along for a while." He frowned. "Lance wasn't an easy guy to be around."

"Why not?" I asked.

"Lucky was a different kind of guy. Jittery." Burrows shook his head. "It was hard to pin him down. He was always looking for that pot of gold at the end of the rainbow."

I couldn't help wondering if he'd found something other than gold at the end of that rainbow. Something that had gotten him killed.

"He liked money," Hal said. It wasn't a question.

Burrows snorted. "Well, yeah. I mean, who doesn't? But this went way beyond a love of scratch.

Lucky would do anything to score. I mean anything. And it got him into trouble all the time." Burrows smiled. There seemed to be a touch of fondness in it. "It was one of the things I liked about him. But it got old after a while. It drew a lot of the wrong kind of attention."

Hal raised his brows. "The police?"

Burrows' grin was slightly mean. "Them too."

"He made enemies in dangerous places?" Hal asked.

"Some, yeah."

"Mr. Burrows, have you heard the name, Garland Medford?"

"Nah. Don't know him." He glanced toward his house. "I need to get back to my ribs."

Hal tugged a card from the pocket of his shirt. "If you think of anything that might help us find Lucky's killer, I'd appreciate a call."

Burrows took it, staring at the tidy white rectangle. "Lucky had a girl." He frowned. "I can't remember her name, Polly something, I think. She might be able to give you more information."

"Any idea where we might find her?" Hal asked.

"Not really. Like I said, I haven't seen Lucky for a while." He turned away and headed for the door, stopping with his hand on it. "You might try his house. Seems to me she was living with him."

"His mom's place?" I asked, frowning.

"No. His place. He has a trailer out by the Fawn

River. It's hidden in a copse of trees along County Road 57. He doesn't own the land. But he's been squatting there for a few years now." He started to go inside and stopped, turning to us. "Look, I know I have a rep, but all that stuff I used to do is in my past. I'm trying to do better. I wouldn't kill Lucky. And I wouldn't steal. I'm keeping my nose clean now."

We climbed back into Hal's car and sat, staring at the duplex for a few minutes. Finally, I said, "He's not as thuggish as I'd thought he would be."

Hal didn't respond for a minute.

"What are you thinking?" I asked, finally.

"We didn't mention stealing that cash." He turned to me. "So why did Burrows bring it up?"

My eyes went wide. I'd totally missed that. "Should we go back and ask him about it?"

"No. Arno should, though." He pushed the ignition button. "He'll need to see if Burrows has an alibi." Backing the car around, he drove out of the duplex complex, heading for Highway 65.

"If Lucky had a home here, why do you suppose he was living at the auction?" I asked Hal.

"That's an excellent question," he responded. "I suspect, like Bobo said, he was hiding. And if that's the case, I'm guessing the person he was hiding from caught up to him at Fulle Proof."

And killed him with a hammer. I shivered violently. "If what George said was true and Lucky had a girlfriend, what are the odds he told her who was after him?"

"I'd say they're pretty good," Hal answered.

I sighed. "That's not good. If Lucky was being stalked and he told his girlfriend about it, then she could be in a lot of danger."

"Yeah," Hal said. "I had the same thought."

7

Arno sent a couple of deputies out to check the river shoreline along County Road 57 where a trailer could be parked. We were notified that they'd located it an hour after speaking to Burrows. The call came from Deputy Schmidt, the newest member of the growing Sheriff's Office and the only female.

Arno put her call on speaker so we could both hear what she had to say. I knew as soon as she started talking that it wasn't good. "Go ahead, Deputy," Hal told the cop. "You have Joey Fulle and me on the line."

"Something definitely went down here," she started. "The trailer's been trashed. The door has been smashed in, and the place was tossed."

"Any sign of the woman we're looking for?" Hal asked.

"No, sir. But we've got blood. Lots of it."

Hal's expression turned sad. "Understood. We're coming over. Can you give me the GPS coordinates for your location, Deputy?"

I knew as soon as Hal stopped the car behind the Sheriff's vehicle that Lucky's luck had well and truly run out. Whatever Lucky had gotten himself into, I had a bad feeling that his girlfriend might have gotten caught in the crossfire.

The streamlined aluminum trailer was something that could be pulled behind a truck. It was a "mobile" home in the true sense of the word.

The sides of the trailer were dented, the metal pocked and cloudy with age.

The single window in the center was broken, a graveyard of pots, dishes, and small appliances littering the ground beneath it.

Broken glass caught the fading sunlight amid the clutter, speckling the destruction with fractured silver light.

The single door was hanging at an awkward angle over the fold-out steps leading up to it. Ruddy smears painted the aluminum in a broken swath along the side.

Deputy Schmidt walked toward us as we climbed out of the big SUV, her dark blue gaze looking haunted despite the neutral set to her attractive features.

She looked to be about five feet nine inches tall and had straight brown hair, which she'd pulled away from her angular face into a glossy bun at the back of her head. The deputy had discarded her hat and pulled on a heavy, uniform jacket against the cold wind scouring the shoreline of the wide river.

Hal offered her his hand. "Deputy, it's a pleasure to finally meet you."

From what Arno had told us, Deputy Schmidt had finished in the top five of her class at the police academy. She was smart, strong, and willing to take on any job to prove herself. I was pretty sure she was going to last longer than the last woman the sheriff had deputized. Like Hal, I'd been looking forward to meeting her too.

I shook her hand, giving it a supportive squeeze. "It's about time we had some girl power in that office."

Schmidt laughed as I'd hoped she would. "I don't know about power, ma'am. So far, all I've managed to do is wrangle my favorite pen back from Deputy Sheppard. Repeatedly."

Hal grinned. "He does have a thing for pens. And he has trouble holding onto them."

"Please," I said, "call me Joey."

She nodded, turning toward the trailer. "As I said

on the phone, there's clear evidence of B&E. Unless the person living here is highly unorganized, I'd say somebody tossed the place looking for something." She started toward the trailer, still talking. "I found bloody handprints on the door and along one wall, as if someone were using the wall to stay on his or her feet. Spatter in the kitchen is representative of a stabbing."

"How so?" I asked, curious.

She skimmed me a look, appearing surprised that I'd asked. "The stains are larger, no misting or high velocity spatter as there would be with a gunshot. There were at least two strikes."

When I lifted my brows, she explained. "There's generally no spatter from the first strike in a stabbing. The fact that there are stains at all tells me the victim was stabbed more than once."

Hal eyed her with respect. "Nice work, Deputy."

Schmidt looked as if she might be offended by his praise, no doubt assuming he was being condescending. It made me sad that she seemed to expect that.

"Hal was a Detective in Indy before he became a PI," I explained to the other woman.

He gave her an apologetic smile. "No offense meant, Deputy. I'm genuinely impressed."

Schmidt flushed with pleasure.

"Any sign of where the victim went after leaving the trailer?"

"No fresh tire tracks. If the perps brought a vehicle, they must have parked it closer to the road." She glanced toward the river. "No sign of fresh foot travel along the river in either direction. No evidence of off-road vehicles."

"A boat?" I asked.

She pointed toward a tree close to the water. There was a short but steep incline between the mostly flat ground where the trailer sat, and the river. "There's a rope tied around that tree, and drag marks at the sandy edge of the water. It's possible there was a boat there at some point."

Hal stared at the tree, giving a brisk little nod. I knew what that nod meant. He intended to check it out further.

I glared at the incline and then frowned down at my sneakers, sighing. There was definitely an embarrassing butt-over-teakettle event in my near future.

Schmidt jerked her head toward the door. "Go on inside and form your own opinions. There are booties and gloves by the door. Please don't step in any evidence or touch anything without gloves."

Hal pulled the rock he'd dug out of Burrows' tire out of his pocket and handed it to Schmidt. "Can you analyze this against the rocks at the Auction lot? It came from George Burrows' bike."

Schmidt nodded. "Will do."

I was certainly no expert in crime scene science. But with Deputy Schmidt's comments fresh in my mind, I had to agree with her main observations. That someone had broken into Lucky Lucklin's trailer. That they'd been looking for something. And that somebody had been attacked there.

Hal stood in front of a short wall running from the end of the kitchen cabinets to the exterior door, which hung at an odd angle from hinges that weren't nearly strong enough to withstand the kind of violent blows I guessed had been used to break inside.

Hal pointed to the door. "I'm guessing the victim fell into the door when she was stabbed and it gave way. She fell out. And took off for the river."

"Those are relatively small handprints," I observed, standing next to Hal.

He nodded. "I'm guessing they belong to a woman." He grimaced, his perfect lips tightening. The Greek god was an old-fashioned guy. He believed women and children were to be protected at all costs. Since he'd been around Caphy and our little band of animals, he'd added animals to that protected list.

He clearly wasn't happy at the idea that a defenseless woman was attacked so brutally in her home.

"These are dangerous people," he told me, without dragging his gaze from the wall.

I nodded, shivering.

Hal wrapped an arm around me, rubbing his hand over my back before moving toward the rear of the trailer home, where a small bedroom held a full-sized bed and a single five-drawer dresser. The covers had all been yanked off the bed and thrown to the floor. The mattress had been tugged off its wooden platform, both sides had been slashed, and its innards had been ripped out.

The dresser drawers hung open, a couple of them broken and hanging askew like the front door. Clothing was strewn over the aged, dark-gold shag carpet, much of it trampled and covered in mud.

Hal pointed to the inexpensive but decidedly feminine underclothing scattered through the mess. "Polly definitely lived here."

I nodded, feeling the cold of despair digging its claws deep into my bones. The destruction felt so personal. So angry. So cold.

Standing in the doorway, I lamented the wanton destruction of someone's personal space.

I heard the swish of a shower curtain and the soft snick of cabinets closing in the nearby bathroom.

Giving in to my rampant porcelain-phobia, I kept my distance as Hal checked out that particular room. I barely managed to deal with my own bathroom spaces. I had no desire to go snooping through someone else's. Besides, I told myself, there wasn't room for two people in the tiny bathroom.

Hal came out a moment later. "The toilet was ripped apart. The contents of the cabinet were thrown around." He shook his head. "Whatever they were looking for, I suspect they didn't find it."

"Why do you think that?" I asked.

He jerked his head toward the broken window in the sleeping area. "Somebody was really mad. People who get what they want generally aren't this angry."

He had a point.

We searched through the storage benches that made up the small dining area, finding nothing but extra blankets and a few personal items. I pulled a torn photo album off the floor beneath the table and sat down to go through it.

Nearly every photo had Lucky Lucklin in it. Several with a man who looked a lot like Lucky. Most likely his dad. A few were of him and his mom at his mom's place. He looked happy in most of the pictures, with the kind of wide grin that seemed to say he was a man with few problems. The more I learned about old Lucky, the more I realized that was unlikely.

There were a few newer photos at the back of the album, they were pictures of Lucky with a woman who was nearly as tall as he was. She was a big girl, strong-looking, with blonde hair and skin that was baked an unhealthy-looking dark brown. Her hair hung in soft waves to mid-back, and she wore it carelessly tousled around her wide face, the strands glossy and thick.

"Polly, I presume?" Hal asked from behind me.

I turned to look up at him. "Maybe?"

"She doesn't look like a pushover," he said, frowning.

I'd had the same thought. Polly Whatshername looked like a woman who could take care of herself. I wondered if she'd been put to the test in the very trailer where I sat.

"Bring one of those pictures with you," Hal said. "If the techs can't discover her identity from DNA in this trailer, we'll show it around in town and to Bobo and Mrs. Lucklin. Maybe we'll get lucky and find somebody who knows her."

I peeled the plastic up and pulled out the last photo in the album, surprised when my fingers grasped a picture that had been printed on computer paper. "It's weird he has an album," I told Hal, holding up the flimsy picture. "Most people these days take pictures on their phones."

Hal nodded. "But those can be lost. He wanted something more permanent. That tells me Lucky cared about this girl."

His words made me sad. I slipped from the booth, carefully sliding the photo into my back pocket, where it would stay fairly flat. "I guess we've put it off as long as we can," I sighed.

Hal laughed, wrapping an arm around my shoulders and tugging me close to kiss me on the temple. "I promise I won't laugh too hard when you fall."

"Har!" I told him, poking him in his rock-hard belly. "Be careful. You could slip too."

He shook his head, lifting a foot to show me the serious tread on his hiking boots. "I planned ahead."

Biting my tongue to keep from sticking it out at him, I trudged out the door ahead of Hal, a woman with bad shoes and something to prove.

It turned out my back pocket probably wasn't the best place to put the paper photo of Lucky and his girl.

By the time I found flatish ground again, my entire backside was wet and muddy. Even my blonde locks were painted in glossy mud.

To his credit, Hal hid the smile trying to escape from his iron control.

Unfortunately, he couldn't do anything about the gleam in his perfect green gaze.

I slapped him on the arm as he pulled me off the ground for the third time, and he grunted happily. We trudged through the mud toward the tree and the telltale rope.

Okay, if I'm being honest, I trudged, Hal moved with his usual liquid grace.

It didn't take him long to find evidence that Polly

had used the boat we suspected had been tied there. He showed me the dark smears of dried blood crusting the rope's fibers. "It's a pretty good bet she made her way downriver. The only question is, did they follow her?" Hal pointed to the mish-mash of footsteps around the tree.

He crouched down and looked at them, his gaze painting a track from the tree to the sandy river's edge. Just inside the water, a dark area showed where someone had stepped in and sunk deep. "Somebody tried to follow her into the river."

I pointed to the tree. "Is that a bullet hole?"

Hal stood again, stepping around the footprints and examining the spot from the side of the tree. "It is. Good eye, Joey." He threw me a grin and then snapped a picture of the bullet hole and the tracks beneath the tree. Finally, getting a pic of the bloody rope.

He sent the pictures to Arno and then slid the phone into his pocket, straightening to look downriver.

Staring at the shoreline tangled with heavy vegetation made my skin itch. The only way to walk along the river in that area was to step close to the water, and that meant sinking into the muck. I grimaced, my teeth grinding together at the thought. "We should probably walk the river to see where she came out, huh?"

Apparently, I didn't hide my despair as well as I'd

thought because he looked at me and grinned. "I think this is a job for Arno's people. Don't you?"

I nearly collapsed with relief. "Yes. I do." I grinned as he threw an arm over my shoulders, looking up the hill toward the trailer.

His next words ripped the smile right off my face.

"Besides, you're probably not going to be much good for any more hiking once you trip and stumble your way back up that hill."

8

More than anything, I hated it when Hal proved me wrong just by being right. He didn't even gloat or act superior when it happened. He was kind and considerate, helping me scrape the inch of mud off my jeans and shirt and carefully laying a clean towel over the seat of his pristine Escalade so I could ride home in mud-glossed comfort.

I hated that about him.

Not really.

By the time Hal pulled into my driveway, the mud had pretty much dried and turned stiff. The worst thing about it was the stench. The aromatic mix of dead fish, rotting vegetation, and other things I didn't want to know about just about made my eyes water.

I really wished it wasn't coming from me.

Hal parked in front of my house and came around to open my door. As he tugged me out, mud crumbled in a small pile on the asphalt drive and withered weeds sifted from my hair. Even the hand he grasped to help me down from the car was crusty with stinky mud.

To his credit, he didn't even grimace.

But I noticed he wiped his hand on his pristine jeans after dropping mine.

I walked stiff-legged and cold toward my front door, navigating the wide steps toward the front porch like a cast member of the Living Dead.

All I was missing was the blank gaze and deep-throated grunt to be a perfect zombie.

I even smelled like a rotting, animated corpse.

Caphy yipped excitedly from inside the house, flinging herself against the door as Hal unlocked it. When he shoved it open, she roared out to see me, offering me a pitty grin, a wildly snapping tail, and an excited whine.

She slammed on her pibl brakes a few feet away and skidded across the wood planking, her eyes wide and her ears flat to her head.

With a long, pitiful whine, my sweet Pitbull changed direction in mid-slide and bounded down the steps, tail tucked and pretty green gaze sliding over her shoulder as she ran to make sure the zombie wasn't trying to eat her.

Great, the pibl who regularly rolled in stinky dead worms had rejected me because of my stench.

"Even my dog hates me," I yodeled pathetically.

To his credit, Hal tried to pull me into a hug. Then he realized I was unhuggable, and settled for a reluctant pat on the back. Even that sent mud spraying into the air around us. "Do you want me to hose you down out here?"

I wasn't sure the full effect of my glare made it through the mud that was caked across my features, but it didn't matter anyway. The gleam was back in his gaze. I knew as soon as I turned my back, he'd be laughing at me.

At least he hadn't run whining into the yard like Caphy.

I toed off my ruined sneakers and trudged inside.

Like the pibl, LaLee took one look at me and put her feline nose into the air, trying to saunter in the opposite direction like she didn't care. But her tiny paws hit the floor a little faster than usual, and she leaped to her "hideout" position on top of the enter-tainment armoire in the living room. High above my head and safely out of mud-crusted reach.

Ethel Squeaks ran squealing from the kitchen, curly tail spinning happily and adorable ears bouncing as she ran. She snuggled up next to me, happily snorfling my stinkiness. "At least Ethel still loves me," I murmured.

Hal nodded. "Of course she does. You're like a

mobile, vertical mud puddle. You're any pig's dream."

I slapped him on the arm, and he gave up trying not to laugh.

I shuffled stiffly away from him, heading for the shower. Ethel trailed contentedly in my wake.

Behind me, Hal apparently thought he needed to make amends. "I'll fix Ethel a snack," he told me, a smile in his deep voice.

I lifted a hand without turning, letting him know I didn't appreciate his good humor at my expense. Ethel escorted me into the shower, grinning. Apparently she thought standing under me as all that lovely mud washed down to the floor of the shower stall was just this side of hog heaven. Pun intended.

I let myself smile and then laugh.

After all, my last arm-spinning, leg pumping, splat and roll down the slimy incline *had* been pretty spectacular.

"We've got a BOLO out on Polly Doe," Arno told us the next morning in his office. I sat in my usual chair in front of his desk and stared past him, to the traffic flashing by in both directions on the nearby highway. Seeing all those people going about their daily lives a quarter of a mile away was both comforting and sad.

To Polly Doe, *normal* was a distant memory. And her new reality showed all the signs of being pretty grim.

"Bobo Biddens has offered to take his bloodhound, Sissy, along the river to see if we can suss out where Polly came out of the water," Arno told us.

Hal's eyebrows rose. "Bobo has a trained tracking dog?"

Arno winced slightly. "Trained is a loose term for Sissy. But she's wicked smart and has the best nose in the county. If that poor woman climbed out of the water anywhere along the river within a couple of miles of the trailer, Sissy will find her."

I refocused my attention on the deputy. "What are the chances we'll find her alive?"

"About sixty forty," he responded with his usual brusque honesty. "She's lost a lot of blood. I can't even imagine how she got down to that boat and launched it. Let alone rowed it up the river for any distance."

"I can answer for the first part," I said, my lips twitching. "I'm sure she slid down to the boat. I can attest to the fact that it's faster that way. If a little hard on the clothes."

Hal chuckled, shaking his head. "Did your crime scene people pull any useful prints from the trailer?"

"That would be Deputy Schmidt. Did I tell you she has a degree in forensic science? That's one of the reasons I hired her. She dug a 22 slug out of that tree. The deputy's processing the prints she collected right now. We should know more later today." He frowned. "Schmidt also tested that piece of rock you gave her. She said it was limestone, consistent with the rock on the auction lot. And there were traces of tractor oil on the piece you gave her. That does seem to point to the auction. But, before you get too excited, most of the gravel in Indiana is crushed limestone, and tractor oil gets spilled on country roads every day."

Nodding, Hal got to his feet, and I followed. "So, not conclusive, but it does keep the possibility open that George Burrows could have been at the auction."

"Yep," Arno agreed.

"I'll drop back by his house and talk to him again," Hal said. Then he said something else that sent icy fingers of doom sliding along my spine. "I'd like to go with Biddens and the bloodhound if that's okay."

Of course he would.

And of course the cranky deputy, who rarely allowed me to stick my pert nose into the evidence-gathering end of his business, would say yes to the Greek god.

Dagnabit!

Heat had settled into the river basin by the time Hal and I arrived back at the trailer. Rain had been misting the area all morning. The combination of heat and moisture had magically created ravenous swarms of mosquitoes to sing us on our way and nibble on every inch of available flesh until I thought I'd go mad from the nasty critters.

Fortunately, I'd listened to Hal, who it turned out had some experience working with tracking dogs. I'd dressed to cover most of my flesh, had donned boots with good tread on them and had liberally sprayed myself down with flower-scented oil that was reputed to be good at repelling the biting pests.

It worked only half as well as I'd hoped it would.

I slapped at another mosquito, sweating profusely underneath the long sleeves of my button-up shirt, and watched with interest as Bobo tried to talk Sissy out of chasing a fat gray rabbit that was fleeing the opposite direction from where we wanted to go.

Finally, he managed to inspire her with Parfum de la Polly, in the form of a soft, red flannel shirt that we pulled from the wreckage of the trailer.

With a deep-throated braying, Sissy finally took off in the right direction, and Hal and I slipped in behind her and the lumbering Bobo.

For a bulky guy, Bobo moved pretty well over the

uneven ground and vegetation-thick woods lining the winding river. Most of the time, I couldn't see the big, sweet bloodhound, except for the swaying leaves of the plants she disturbed along her erratic path.

Following Hal's sure steps, I watched Bobo's wide, rounded shoulders beneath his sweat-darkened shirt. Despite the distance and vegetation, we had no trouble following the sound of the hound panting and sniffing her way along the bank.

It also wasn't hard to realize when she finally found something, about an hour into the search.

Her howling bark, sounding like a cross between a moose and a camel, filled the air with a joy that made me smile, despite my discomfort. Bobo stepped out of the trees after her and I could hear his deep voice congratulating the dog, and the soft sound of him affectionately patting her heaving sides.

I was the last to step out of the trees and into the open area surrounding a fast-moving creek. The waterway ran perpendicular to the much wider river, its shallow curves winding through the otherwise wooded area along a tall ridge peppered with dark, misshapen hollows that looked like coyote dens.

Sissy was standing in the creek. Her long legs were immersed up to her knees, and her head was down as she thirstily slurped up the cool, clear water. The tips of her big ears floated on the water's surface as she drank. It made me smile.

Bobo stood in front of me, mopping his head with a plaid handkerchief that looked like it had been soaked in the creek.

Hal was crouched over something caught on the rocky edge of the shallow water. I hurried over, maneuvering around an unmoving Bobo, and stared down at what looked like a denim shirt. Most of it was submerged in the creek, the water a constant barrage against the lightweight blue fabric, making it dance in the swirls and eddies. But one sleeve and part of one side was above the waterline, caught on a tiny scrub tree. Where the water hadn't washed it away, the fabric was stiff with blood.

"Do you think that's hers?" I asked.

Hal looked up at me and finally straightened, his intense green gaze scouring the area. "If it's not we have more than one victim to worry about. That's a lot of blood."

I nodded, slipping my gaze over the agitated river nearby. The rain had caused it to pick up its paces and it was moving along at quite a clip, the foamy water bouncing off partially submerged rock and eddying around fallen tree trunks.

Something bobbed in the midst of a tangle of tree debris near the center of the river. I pointed. "That looks like a rowboat."

Hal nodded, clearly having already noticed it. "I'm guessing she managed to bring it into the intersection where the creek meets the river and stumble out of it. The current must have plucked it back up."

Bobo pointed a thick finger toward a white rectangle I could barely see through the trees. "If she followed this creek, she might have headed there."

A residence. Nestled in the woods and very private. It would probably look like a safe haven to a woman running from a killer. Without another word, Bobo reintroduced the scent-object we'd retrieved from Lucky's trailer to Sissy.

She snuffled it excitedly and started sniffing her way along the water, ending up at the edge of the creek. With a happy howl and a flop of her oversized ears, she picked up the scent and took off running again, heading along the creek's edge toward the home in the distance.

W e found the first signs of blood on the flagstone-lined steps leading out of the woods. The grass at the end of the path was long, almost knee-high, and it was the first clue we had that the home was either vacant or was only used at certain times during the year.

Hal stopped at the top of the path and pointed to a mashed area in the overlong grass. "It looks like something was lying there."

Bobo managed to grab Sissy before she

wandered over and checked it out. "Could be deer?" he offered.

Hal moved closer, taking care to stay off the trail of mashed grass leading to the larger area. He crouched down and pointed. "There's blood."

I peered over his shoulder, seeing the smeared evidence of our fleeing victim on the wide-bladed grass. "Polly fell."

Hal frowned and stood. "She's getting weak from blood loss. Frankly, I'm amazed she made it this far."

Clearly, Lucky's girlfriend is a strong, capable girl. Or just a desperate one. After thinking about it for a moment, I decided it was probably a bit of both. "There's more blood," Bobo said, Sissy lunging to escape his grip.

Hal pointed toward the dirt at the edge of the grass, where the woods had been cultivated away to create the small back yard. "Stay off the grass as much as you can," he told us. He quickly called Arno and told him what we'd found. "I can't tell you where we are, we're at the back of the property, and we came up from the river. But you can get the coordinates by tracking my phone." He listened for a beat and then nodded. "We'll see you in a few."

He glanced at Bobo and me. "He wants us to stay out of the house. He's on his way."

Bobo nodded his big head. "I'll take Sissy around front and watch for Arno," he said.

We crept along the edge of the woods, eyes

peeled to the mashed trail leading toward the back of the home. It curved quickly, heading right for the wood door in the center of the white, clapboard wall.

When we reached the corner of the house, Bobo kept going straight, toward the front yard. Staying close to the house so as not to disturb the grass pathway, Hal and I followed along the back wall.

The back door had no concrete pad in front of it. But the grass trail was clear, ending in a trampled space that told us Polly had spent a few moments there, probably looking in the window trying to figure out if anybody was home.

Hal pointed to the pitted brass door handle. It was smeared with blood. There was also blood smeared along the clapboard siding to the side of the door, and the path continued on along the back of the house.

We turned the corner and saw a broken window and a more blood smudges, where it looked like Polly had climbed through.

Hal peered through the window and sighed. "She's on the floor." He pulled out his cell again. "She's not moving."

The sound of sirens cut the stark silence that had been broken only by the occasional chirp of a happy bird and the distant drone of the raging river.

Hal put his cell phone away, pointing toward the front. "Let's go tell Arno what we found and get out of his way."

9

I sat on the front passenger seat of the Escalade, turned sideways with the door open so I could watch the action at the little house. Luckily, Hal had thought to ask Arno to have the car brought to the house so we could leave under our own steam when we were ready.

The ambulance had arrived minutes after Arno and Deputy Schmidt had. They'd carted Polly away on a gurney about twenty minutes later.

Against all odds, she was still alive. Though I'd never met the woman, I felt like I'd gotten to know her a bit through the pictures in Lucky's album and in observing the gutsy, determined path of her escape.

Polly Whatshername was an admirable woman, and I looked forward to meeting her face-to-face.

Hal came out of the house and strode toward me,

his confident, ground-eating strides quickly closing the distance.

I lifted my brows as he approached, a silent request for information.

"She's stable. She's already on IV and they've taken her to DH General."

I knew from working with my PI that he meant Deer Hollow General Hospital, which was about thirty minutes away. "Are we going to speak to her," I asked hopefully.

Hal shook his head. "She'll be going into surgery. Arno's going to speak to her this afternoon if she's awake and aware."

"How bad are her wounds?"

"A few defensive wounds in her hands and fore-arm. The one on her left side is deeper. The EMTs didn't think it was life-threatening. She was lucky. The knife missed all the vital stuff." He frowned. "It's a bad place to have that kind of damage, it's gonna hurt like the dickens, but it could be worse."

"Where to now?" I asked, absently scratching a massive mosquito bite on the side of my sweaty neck.

Hal's green gaze softened. "Home for showers? Arno's going to call us in a couple of hours to discuss next steps. Hopefully, he'll have talked to Polly by then and will know more about what her attackers wanted."

I nodded, shifting to face forward so Hal could close my door.

As we drove toward home, my mind kept spinning over the same questions. What did all this have to do with Lucky Lucklin being murdered at Fulle-Proof Auctions? Why had he been there? How had he gotten a key? And had the person who'd killed him done it before or after Polly had been attacked?

I made a decision. Turning to Hal, I asked, "Would you mind stopping at the auction before we go home?"

Hal lifted a midnight eyebrow in surprise. But he nodded. "Of course. What are you thinking?"

I shrugged. "I'm not sure. I just keep coming back to the same question. Why was he there?"

My cell phone rang as Hal pulled up to the gate. He took the key I handed him and got out to unlock it as I answered. "Hello?"

"Joey, I'm glad I caught you, I was wondering if it was okay to show the property tomorrow?"

Watching Hal push the gate wide, my mind tried to grasp something that kept dancing away from me. I frowned, caught in the thought that it was something important. Still, it wouldn't come.

"Joey?" Madge Watson nudged.

I blinked myself out of my thoughts. "Sorry, Madge. I was distracted watching Hal," I told her, then winced as I realized how that had sounded.

Her laugh was husky with innuendo. "I can't say I blame you there, sweetie."

My answering laugh was brief, insincere. "You want to show the auction lot? Already?" I cleared my throat against the slightly hysterical tone coating my words.

"Yes! Do you believe it? I have a client in Indianapolis who I've worked with on several properties. He just called me out of the blue today, asking about it. He wants to drive down in the morning. Do you think the police would be okay with showing it?"

Hal climbed into the SUV and looked a question at me. I must have appeared pale and shocked. "Hold on, Madge," I said. Pressing the Mute button, I told Hal what she wanted.

He thought about it a moment. "That depends if they're done processing the scene. My guess is that they are, but she'll need to check with Arno."

I passed his recommendation on to Madge, assuring her it was okay with me if it was all right with Arno. Then I disconnected and sat staring out the window, feeling a bit shell-shocked.

"I thought I'd have more time," I told him, my throat closing around the words.

Hal reached over and clasped my hand. His grip was warm and strong, an anchor in the chaos. "You don't have to sell it, honey. You're still in control."

I nodded, swallowing hard. "I know." And I did.

On some level. But I couldn't shake the feeling that I hadn't really been in control for a very long time.

It was a decidedly unsettling thing.

"Where did you want to go?"

I thought about it for a moment and then said, "Let's take a look at the scene of the crime. Maybe Arno or his new crime scene wonder girl missed something."

If he doubted the possibility, Hal didn't show it. Without a word, he nodded and fell in beside me.

We entered the large auction building, the familiar scents hitting me again, but not quite as hard as the last time. Maybe with enough time and exposure, the nostalgia weighing me down would dissipate enough to allow me to actually sell the old place.

It didn't seem likely. Although, knowing a brutal murder had happened in the spot did help me take steps toward that possibility.

Crime scene tape crisscrossed the connecting door between the main auction building and the annex. Hal carefully tugged it off one side and opened the door, pushing it wide as the familiar stench of death and disuse assailed us.

I covered my nose but didn't rock back on my heels like last time. Baby steps. Grimacing at the thought, I realized that I'd have to clean up the blood and air the annex out if I was going to let

Madge show it. I certainly wasn't looking forward to that little task.

Hal preceded me into the room. His intense green gaze slid around the room, seeming to check it for potential trouble before sliding toward the spot where blood still stained the concrete. He pulled a small but powerful flashlight from his pocket and shined it over the space. The small arc of white light illuminated the sticky red-brown stain on the floor and a lot of spider webs. The surface of the wood tool cabinet still showed the distinct shapes of things that had been stored there within the layer of dust.

Hal carefully ran the light over the surface of the cabinet, the surrounding wall, and down to the floor. He got down on his knees and shone it along the dusty concrete.

"Do you see anything?" I asked, hopefully.

"A dead mouse."

I grimaced.

He stood and ran the flashlight along the bottom edge of the drywall where the tool cabinet ended. In some spots, the floor must have been uneven, creating narrow gaps between the concrete and the unpainted drywall.

Something flashed from one of those gaps.

Hal slid the light away, I stopped him with a touch to the shoulder. "No, wait. Scan it back that way." I pointed to the gap and he shone the flashlight there. The tiniest speck of red showed beneath the drywall. "What is that?" I asked.

I tried to dig it out with a fingernail, but it wouldn't budge. Hal looked up at me. "Can you find me a box cutter or a flathead screwdriver?"

I searched through a rolling metal toolbox looking for a knife and not finding one. "I can't believe there's not a single box cutter in here," I said in frustration.

"Wait a minute," Hal said. "I forgot I had this." He showed me his utility knife, and I started to turn as something thumped against the small window over the tool bench. I jumped, giving a little shriek, and then saw the birds fluttering around outside the glass.

I sucked air into my lungs, mentally berating myself for being so jumpy.

Hal sliced the drywall around the object and used the tip of the knife to dig the wall board out. When he'd made himself enough space, he used the tip of the knife to capture the red, plastic object and tug it loose.

Sliding the knife through the metal loop on the end, he held it up for me to see.

It was a keychain. The words "Deer Hollow Realty" were printed across the red plastic.

"How'd that get in there?" I asked, confused.

"Maybe we found the source of the key Lucklin used," Hal said.

Another thump against the glass had me jumping and clutching my chest. A shadow danced across the glass, the silhouette shaped like fluttering wings. "Stupid birds. I wonder what's got them so riled up out there?"

Hal's gaze slid over the room, past the big tractor that was half-covered in a tarp. He shoved the key chain into his pocket.

A fresh breeze slid over us, and my eyes went wide.

There was a crash, followed by a whoosh and the bright flare of flame as it ate up a pile of tarps stacked near the door.

Hal screamed, "Down!" He grabbed my arm and yanked me toward the back of the room, behind the big old tractor.

I was crouched on the floor, Hal wrapped around me, as the initial noise faded out of my consciousness, leaving behind the whoosh and crackle of fire and the stench of acrid smoke sliding through the building.

Hal tucked a finger under my chin and looked me in the eye. "You okay?"

I nodded, coughing against the growing wall of smoke.

"We need to get out of here," he told me, grasping my hand. "Stay low and don't let go of my hand, okay?"

I must have looked terrified because he took a

10

I jumped up and started running, heading in the direction of the shots I'd heard. Two more shots rang out before I reached the big door at the end of the building. I tugged on it, digging my heels into the dirt as the enormous metal door tried to resist my efforts. Finally, I managed to drag it open enough to squeeze through and stopped, peering around the lot in search of Hal.

I saw a dark head bobbing along behind an enormous piece of farm equipment. *Hal!* He was still moving under his own steam.

"Hal!" I shouted, then jumped back with a yelp as a bullet sheared through the thin metal siding inches from my shoulder.

"Stay down and stay back!" Hal yelled.

Not likely, I thought, scoping out my options in the yard.

Most of the equipment had been retrieved from the yard when my parents were declared dead. But a few pieces, like the huge, rusted hulk of the elderly harvester Hal was currently hiding behind, apparently hadn't been worth the time and money for its owners to retrieve.

Other items, like the John Deere utility vehicle that was parked a few feet away, had belonged to the auction. I eyed the UV, memories sliding through me as I recalled the first time dad had let me drive it around the lot all by myself.

Another shot exploded in the distance, the bullet banging loudly off the metal harvester and forcing Hal to throw himself to the ground to avoid the rebounding slug.

My heart banging against my ribs, I tried to find where the shooter was perched, seeing nothing through the rising smoke and the scattered corpses of abandoned equipment.

A flare of muzzle flash blossomed through the smoke. It had come from behind a small storage shed about twenty yards away from Hal.

"Gotcha," I murmured, then, crouching lower, I made a run for the utility vehicle.

Bullets rained around me, followed quickly by answering fire from Hal.

Grabbing a concrete block from a pile near the building, I made good use of the cover fire he gave me and jumped into the UV, flinging the block to the passenger seat.

Quickly turning the key, I shoved the utility vehicle into gear. I turned in the direction of the shooter and slammed my foot down on the pedal. Holding the steering wheel to keep it moving in the right direction, I ducked sideways as the small vehicle plowed a direct path to the corner of the shed where the shooter was hunkered down.

Bullets pinged loudly off the front of the vehicle. One of them pierced the plexiglass windshield, ripping through the back of the seat where I was sitting. If I'd been sitting up, it would have killed me.

It was time to abort.

I grabbed the concrete block with two hands, hoping the UV held to its course, and pulled my foot off the gas, replacing it with the block.

The utility vehicle charged past the harvester. I caught a glimpse of Hal, his handsome face dark with worry, as I shoved off the seat and threw myself free of the vehicle, rolling over the hard-packed ground until I was behind the harvester.

Hal fired toward the shed again, rushing toward me as he stopped. "Are you okay?"

I nodded, shoving myself off the ground.

He put his hand on my head. "Stay down. I swear, Joey. You're going to be the death of me."

Ignoring his chastising, I peered over the top of the rusted hulk of metal. The UV was heading straight for the shed, and the shooter was still firing at it. With the smoke hanging heavy in the air, he couldn't tell that I wasn't still inside.

Sirens sheared through the day, sounding slightly muffled inside the thick curtain of smoke.

Hal grabbed my hand and pulled me to the body of the giant-sized implement, where the engine gave us more substantial protection.

"Did you see who it was?" I asked hopefully.

"No. Between the smoke and the fact that he keeps ducking behind stuff, all I know is that he's a decent shot with that rifle and he's pretty determined."

I nodded. "The police are here."

Hal's gaze slipped toward the burning outbuildings. "Hopefully, the fire department too."

I nodded, but I didn't really care about the buildings. They could be repaired or replaced.

Hal was safe. That was the important thing.

I heard the UV connect with the shed and lifted my head. "Shooting's stopped."

He nodded. "He'd be stupid to hang around with the police here."

"What do you think he wanted?" I asked, frowning.

"No idea. But he's definitely gotten my attention. And I'm going to find out."

The annex was pretty much totaled. The tractor that had been inside was a charred hulk, only the metal remaining. The one positive was that it hadn't blown up. There must not have been any or much fuel in the thing.

"The main building was barely damaged," Hal told me, probably trying to get the scowl off my face.

I could tell from his manner that he was worried about my emotional state. But I wasn't sad. I was mad. Big difference. One of those two emotions took me off my feet, sending me to bed. The other one energized me and made me more determined to find out what was going on.

Arno walked over to Hal and me, his handsome face dark with unhappiness. He shook his head. "I'm really sorry about this, Joey."

I blinked, unaccustomed to the cranky lawman being nice to me.

"Oh. Um. Yeah, thanks."

Seemingly as uncomfortable with his kind words as I was, he looked at Hal. "I understand you exchanged gunfire with the person who started this?"

Hal inclined his head, his arms crossed over his chest. He wore an expression that didn't bode well for somebody. He was mad. "Yes. Tall guy. Had one of those ski masks on. Black pants, black turtleneck, black shoes. Good with a rifle."

"When you say *good,* do you mean...?"

"Formally trained," Hal clarified.

Arno winced. "I'm sorry to hear that."

Hal nodded. "He seemed to know his way around the complex." He considered for a minute, then lifted his gaze to Arno. "I found a spot at the very back where the fencing was cut."

I made a small sound of anger. More damage for me to fix. I couldn't wait to find the guy so I could show him my appreciation.

Hal gave me a commiserating look.

"Do you think he was looking for anything specific?"

"I'm not sure if that was it. Or if he just saw that we were here and took advantage of the opportunity. He could have assembled that cocktail with stuff on this lot. It wasn't fancy but it certainly did the trick," Hal said. "He either he wanted us dead..."

"Or he didn't know you were in there and was just destroying evidence," Arno finished for him. "We went over that building with a fine-tooth comb after Mr. Lucklin's murder," Arno said. "Any evidence that was there, we've already collected."

Hal pulled the key chain out of his pocket, holding it up by the ring for Arno to see. "Not everything."

Arno frowned. "Where'd you find that?" He pulled a latex glove out of his pocket and took the key with it, frowning when he saw the realtor's logo. "I guess that explains where Lucklin got the key."

I nodded. "But Madge wouldn't have given it to him," I said. "Has she recently reported a break-in?" I asked.

"Not that I know of. I can check when I get back, but..."

"But it would be easier to just ask," Hal said, nodding. "We'll go talk to her if you don't mind."

Which reminded me. "Did she call to ask you if she could have a showing?" When Arno's brows lifted, I added. "It was before this happened, of course."

"She didn't. I'm surprised she has a potential buyer already. Who is it?"

"Somebody from Indy," I said.

"Indy, huh? That could be important."

"She said he's been a client for a while." I offered.

Arno thought about it for a minute and glanced at Hal. "See if you can get the client's stats. If she won't give them to you, I'll call her. The timing of this is very suspicious."

"Agreed," Hal said.

"How's Polly?" I asked the cop.

"I was heading over there when I got the call about your fire." He scanned another look toward the smoldering remains of the annex. "I'm going to be here a while. I'm waiting for a fire investigator from Bloomington."

"You want us to speak to Polly?" Hal asked.

"Joey might want to stick around here," Arno said, his words as much a question as a statement.

Both men looked at me. I shook my head. "There's nothing I can do to help. I'd rather be trying to find this guy."

Arno nodded. "Then, if you wouldn't mind getting Polly's statement, that would help a lot. I'm not sure how much you'll be able to get out of her. She could still be kind of loopy from the pain meds."

"Don't worry about that," I told the deputy. "I'll find a way to get through to her. This guy's gotten on my last nerve and I'm over it."

Arno snickered. "Okay. But no waterboarding the victim."

"I'm not making any promises," I grumbled back.

And I was only about half kidding.

11

Madge was just unlocking the office when Hal parked in her small gravel lot. She smiled and waved when she spotted us, leaving the door open behind her as she disappeared inside.

Climbing out of the car, I wrapped my arms around myself and shivered. We'd stopped by home to shower and change and my long blonde hair was still damp.

The air had grown much cooler since that morning. It had felt like a hot summer day down by the river.

Hal reached into the back of the SUV and pulled out a jacket, draping it over my shoulders.

I looked down at the IMPD logo on the leather coat, inhaling the dual scents of leather and Greek god. "Thank you."

He inclined his head. "Are you sure you don't want to go back home? It's been a crazy day."

Understatement of the year.

I shook my head. "I'm fine. It's just gotten chilly since the clouds moved in." I glanced skyward. "Looks like there's a storm coming."

He nodded. "You ready?"

In response, I started down the sidewalk leading toward the Realtor's sagging front porch. It had been a while since I'd visited Madge at the office, but a quick assessment told me nothing much had changed.

The sign hanging from a metal arm attached to one of the two columns on either side of the steps was still dented, the black letters of the business name pitted and slightly crooked.

The porch boards were still warped, the stain long since worn off, and the cracked mortar still hadn't been repaired, giving the building a sagging appearance on one end.

I knew Madge was struggling to make a go of it in Deer Hollow. She'd lost her partner soon after they'd opened the office and had still to find someone to take Penney's place. To be honest, I was a little surprised she hadn't just closed up shop and returned to Indianapolis. Opportunities to grow her client list would have to be better in the larger city by a magnitude of ten.

Madge was pouring coffee into a mug that bore

the Deer Hollow Realtor logo on the front when we came inside. She gave me a smile. "Coffee?"

"That would be wonderful, thanks."

She handed me the mug and pointed to the fixings arrayed on the tidy counter next to the coffee maker. "Help yourself to sugar and cream." She glanced at Hal. "How about you?"

"Please?"

A few moments later, Madge motioned to the small conference room off the lobby. I was pretty sure it had once been a bedroom, but the wall over-looking the lobby had been fitted with a large interior window, so Madge still had a sight-line to the main area when she was meeting with clients.

She sat down with a weary sigh.

"Busy day?" I asked, smiling.

"Yes, actually." Madge's grin was wider than usual. And despite the arcs beneath her eyes that spoke of her weariness, she looked happy. "I've sold a handful of properties in the new subdivision this month."

"That's great," I said, meaning it.

She nodded. "Business is finally picking up. And if I can sell your place, I might even be able to afford some updates to the office."

I bristled at her statement before realizing she'd been talking about the auction, not my home. That was a sensitive subject with me. Her partner Penney had been obnoxious about trying to sell my house out from under me. If she hadn't managed to get herself killed not too long after she invaded my private space and all but demanded that I let her list it, she and I had been on a collision course for a real blowout about it.

"That's why we're here," Hal said, skimming me a quick look. "I'm afraid there's been a...development."

Madge's eyes went wide. "What kind of development?"

"Someone started a fire in the annex building and took a few potshots at us," I said.

Madge's mug hit the table with a thud. "Pot shots? You mean they shot at you?"

"Yeah."

"Holy Humperdinck!" She shook her head. "You're okay, though?"

I appreciated that she asked about our health before she worried about the loss of a potential sale. Her partner definitely wouldn't have had the same priorities.

"We're fine. Thanks to some James-Bond-like maneuvers by Joey with a utility vehicle," Hal said, grinning at me.

I flushed with embarrassment. "Heat of the moment. I lost my mind a little." I didn't want to tell him the reason I'd lost my mind was because he was in danger.

"You'll have to tell me about that, sometime,"

Madge said, patting my hand. "But I'm guessing that's not why you're here."

"The damage to the annex is complete," I told her, grimacing. "The main building has only minor damage. I'll get that repaired."

She nodded. "I'll crunch the numbers, and we can adjust the price accordingly."

"That's fine," Hal said. "But, I'm afraid the auction is going to be unavailable for showings until the police figure out what our shooter was doing there."

Her dark brows lowered unhappily. "Oh. I see. That's unfortunate."

"I'm sure your buyer from Indy will be okay with waiting," I told her. "There won't be any danger of anybody buying it out from under him."

She didn't look convinced. Chewing on her lower lip, Madge ran her fingers over her mug, her concern clear on her face.

"What can you tell us about this buyer?" Hal asked softly.

Madge looked surprised for a beat, and then realization pinkened her cheeks with affront. "You think he had something to do with this? That's crazy. Why would he damage something he wanted to buy?"

Off the top of my head, I could think of one reason. "To get a better price?" I suggested.

Madge blew out an exasperated sigh. "That's a

little extreme, don't you think? Tony's got more money than a Washington politician. He'd never consider trying to slash the price that way." Her lips curved in a wry smile. "He wouldn't be above haggling mercilessly, though. I fully expect that."

"Okay, assuming he wouldn't pull the stunt to get Joey to lower her price, what will his response to this new wrinkle be?"

Madge caught Hal's gaze and straightened in her chair, her chin coming up in reproach. But it only took her a moment to deflate. The color deepened in her cheeks as she sighed. "He'll want a slash in the price."

I didn't think Hal had been trying to prove my point, but he'd done it nicely nonetheless.

"I've known Tony Baxter almost my entire career," Madge said. "He's a tough businessman, but fair. There's never been a hint of anything illegal. He's a good man."

"Why is he interested in the auction property?" Hal asked.

"He's made his millions in warehousing goods. My understanding is that he's going to put a couple of warehouses on the property."

"Then, he'll be tearing everything down?" I asked, surprisingly offended by the prospect.

Madge flushed again, unable to meet my eyes. "I believe so, yes."

I fell silent, secretly hoping the man chose to look elsewhere for his warehousing plot.

"Arno is going to want all the information on your client," Hal told the realtor.

She lowered her gaze, scraping a lock of messy brown hair off her cheek. "I'll call him before I leave today."

Hal reached into his pocket and pulled out the keychain we'd found. Arno had given him an evidence baggie for it before we left the lot.

Placing it on the table between Madge and us, he asked, "Is this one of yours?"

Madge frowned, reaching for it. "That's one of my new ones, with the bigger logo."

"How new?" Hal asked.

I knew what he was asking. If she'd gotten the keychains within the last few weeks or even months, it would have been highly unlikely for it to end up at the auction unless Lucky had brought it.

"They arrived a couple of weeks ago," Madge answered. Her fingers hovering above the bag, she jerked her gaze to his. "Where did you find this?"

"At a murder scene."

Madge lost the flush she'd gotten when speaking about her client and then some, turning pasty with shock. "Yikes! You don't think that I..."

"We're not accusing you of anything," I told her soothingly. "But the police were wondering where the victim got a key to the lot. It looks like he might have gotten it from you."

Madge's fingers twisted together and she leaned back in her chair, her expression tense. "I don't..." She sighed, rubbing a hand over her eyes. "I thought I'd misplaced it."

"What happened?" I asked.

"I can't be everywhere at once," she started and then stopped, shaking her head. "That's an excuse. I screwed up. The key was on my desk and I left the woman alone upfront while I used the printer."

"What woman?" Hal and I asked at the same time.

"She claimed she was looking for a home in Deer Hollow. I offered to show her what I had available in her price range. She agreed, seemed excited. But when I went back to get the listings off the printer, she left. I heard the front door close and came back out here. She was gone and..." Madge turned a tearful gaze on me. "I didn't notice it until later, but the key for your property was gone off my desk."

"How would she have known what the key was for?" Hal asked.

"I had it sitting with the listing. When she said she was looking to buy I picked it up to move it, then..." she sighed. "I'm afraid I made a joke, asking her if she wanted to buy a home with a hundred acres."

"What was her name?" Hal was already pulling his phone out of his pocket.

"She didn't give it to me. We hadn't gotten that far."

"What did she look like?" I asked.

"Big woman. Thirties. Tan. She had beautiful hair. Blonde."

Hal and I shared a look.

Polly.

"When did this happen?" he asked, shoving to his feet.

"A week ago." Madge stood too, all the color draining from her face. "Please tell me that wasn't your killer?"

"We're not sure," Hal said, offering Madge a quick smile. "We'll let you know when the property can be shown again. Okay?"

Madge winced, nodding.

As we headed out of the conference room, she called my name.

I stopped and turned back. "Yes?"

"I'm so sorry, Joey."

"No worries," I told her, trying to sound sincere. "It's not your fault."

"It is. I'll take ownership. I screwed up. But, on a happier note, I wanted to thank you for your recommendations. I think I might have someone lined up."

"That's wonderful!" I told her. "Keep me posted on that, will you?"

Hal held the front door open for me and followed me out. "What recommendations?"

"She asked me if I knew of anybody who might like to become a realtor. I gave her a few names."

He nodded. "Good. She's got her hands full. And despite trying to remain positive, I can tell it's wearing on her."

I certainly couldn't disagree with him on that.

We decided to stop by George Burrow's place again before heading to the hospital. When Hal pulled into the driveway of the duplex, Burrows was bent over his motorcycle, fiddling with something in the engine. He straightened when he saw us coming and stood watching as Hal parked the SUV.

We climbed out of the car.

George scowled at us, rubbing oily hands on a rag that was already pretty saturated with the stuff. "What do you two want now?"

Such a warm greeting. Be still my heart.

Hal didn't offer Burrows his hand. I wasn't sure if it was because of the less-than-friendly greeting or the grease. He nodded toward the motorcycle. "Engine problems?"

Burrows followed his glance. "Nah. Just giving it a little tune-up."

"I just had a couple more questions for you, Mr. Burrows," Hal said.

Burrows waited, his expression unfriendly.

"What were you doing at Fulle-Proof Auctions?"

Burrows blinked in surprise. Some of the hostility fell away as color leeched from his face. "You spyin' on me, Amity?"

Well, that answered that.

Hal gave him a tight smile. "I don't have the resources to do that. But I'm investigating a murder. Your whereabouts have put you in line for questioning. Please answer the question."

Burrows threw the rag on top of a shiny black tool chest. "That's where Lucky was killed?"

Stupid question. Unless Burrows didn't listen to the local news or read the local paper, which, I realized was a possibility but not likely, he'd know exactly where Lucky's body had been found.

"Let's not waste each other's time, Mr. Burrows," Hal said. "If you continue to play games, I'll be forced to inform Deputy Willager that you need to be brought in for questioning."

Burrows put his hands on his hips and cocked a leg, looking thoughtful. After a long moment, he expelled air. "I didn't kill Lucky."

As good as an admission, and alarming. How many people had been gallivanting all over my property? "Are you saying you were there?" I asked him.

"Once. Just for a minute." He shook his head as if

frustrated by having to explain himself. "I ride on those roads. They're long and straight, and I enjoy the scenery. About a week ago, I saw Lucky at the gate of the auction. I stopped to talk to him because it had been a minute since I'd seen him. I just wanted to say hi and ask him what he was doing at the auction."

"What did he say?"

"He said he was checkin' on it for a friend. I didn't really believe him. Lucky always had an angle on everything, but he wouldn't come off his story."

"What happened then?" Hal asked.

"Then he asked me if I'd seen my sister lately. I thought it was a strange question. Still do. But he was lookin' at me like he suspected me of something. Tell ya the truth, it kind of hacked me off. So I told him he was an a..." He glanced at me. "I told him my sister was too good for him and that he'd better not be trying to drag her into trouble. Lucky just laughed."

"Then?" Hal nudged.

"Then, I left. I didn't give it another thought until you came ta see me."

"What kind of car was he driving?" Hal asked.

George frowned. "What do you mean?"

"I mean, what did his car look like"

"That tan piece of crap Chevy he had? It looked like it always did. Maybe more beat up than usual."

"Could you tell if he was going in or out of the lot," Hal asked.

"The car was pointed toward the gate."

Hal crossed his arms, his eyes narrowing. "Mr. Burrows, the last time we were here, you said you wouldn't steal anything. Why did you say that?"

The other man blinked, looking confused. "I... probably because you told me Lucky stole something."

"No. We didn't tell you that."

Burrows held his gaze for a long moment and then looked away, shrugging. "I know what Lucky's like. I probably just assumed it."

And we all know what assuming does, don't we?

Silence throbbed between the two men for a long moment and then Hal said, "Thank you very much, Mr. Burrows. We'll be in touch." He turned without another word and headed for the Escalade.

I waited until we were inside the car to ask "Did that tell you anything?"

Hal started the car and turned to look over his shoulder as he backed it out of the drive. "It verifies the timeline for when Lucky arrived at the auction."

"But it doesn't clear George Burrows," I said. "We know he was at the auction. He could have killed Lucky."

"He could have. We don't have any real physical evidence against him, though."

"Then that was a complete waste of time," I said, flopping back in my seat.

"Not a waste. It's another piece of the puzzle that will eventually help us put it all together. And it verifies the timing of what Madge told us."

He was right. If Lucky was seen at the gate a week ago, and the key to the auction went missing a week ago, that tracked. "You're right." It was another piece of the puzzle. How important a piece remained to be seen. There was a big difference between a five-hundred-piece puzzle and a three-thousand-piece puzzle.

And I was increasingly starting to worry we were dealing with the latter.

12

We were quiet on the way to the hospital. I didn't know what Hal was thinking, but my thoughts about Polly Whatshername had shifted slightly. I'd gone from seeing her as a victim of the current mess, to someone who might be involved with helping to create the chaos.

As we pulled into the hospital parking lot, I turned to Hal. "If she hadn't been at the hospital, I'd be wondering right now if the shooter at Fulle-Proof could have been Polly."

"Yeah." Hal frowned. "Whoever it was had a head covering that disguised his...or her...hair. It's possible it could have been a woman."

I nodded. "That's what I was thinking too. But why would she kill Lucky?"

"That's what we need to find out. Hopefully, Miss Polly will be willing to talk to us."

Hal opened the car door for me and gave me a hand down. I glanced at his watch and frowned. "We need to get home and feed Ethel Squeaks. She's going to think she's dying."

Hal snorted. "I don't know about you, but I'm gaining a new understanding of the term, 'eat like a pig'."

Arno had called ahead and cleared the way for us to visit Polly Doe, as the information desk had her listed. The woman behind the desk buzzed us through with instructions for how to get to the recovery rooms.

The nurses' station for the recovery department was an island in the center of chaos. Long counters with faux wood fronts formed two L-shaped stations, behind which several nurses worked on computers. A woman in a doctor's white lab coat looked over one nurse's shoulder, speaking softly as we approached.

The nurse and physician both looked up as we stopped in front of them, the doctor giving us a weary smile. "Can I help you?"

Hal showed her his PI credentials and explained we were helping the Sheriff's department by interviewing Ms. Doe.

"I'm Doctor Phillips. You can call me Doc Janna." She smiled, offering him her hand. Hal accepted the offer, and she shook his hand with brisk efficiency.

"She hasn't given you her name yet?" Hal asked.

The doctor frowned. "She says she can't remember it."

Hal arched a brow.

The doctor gave him a commiserating look. "She had no ID on her. We had to take her at her word."

"But why would she lie?" I asked.

The physician skimmed an assessing look over me, probably wondering what my role was. "It's possible she's not lying."

I didn't believe that. Something on my face must have given me away.

She sighed. "We can't bill her if we don't know who she is." Doc Janna placed a hand on the nurse's shoulder. "Tammy, where's the Doe file?"

The dark-haired nurse pulled a tidy pile of clipboards over and sifted through them before pulling one from the center of the stack and handing it to the physician.

The doctor quickly flipped through the top sheets of paper and nodded. "Her pain meds should be wearing off soon. She'll be tired but fairly coherent right now."

"Good," Hal said. "Can you tell us anything about her injuries?"

"Three wounds, two superficial, one fairly deep." She sliced a finger across her side in illustration. "The repair was straightforward. She should be fine in a couple of weeks."

"Did she tell you what happened?"

"No. She was unconscious when she arrived and was taken into surgery right away. She's been heavily medicated since coming out of surgery. I haven't been in to see her for about an hour."

Hal nodded. "Thanks, Doc. Can we go in now?"

"Yes. But only for a couple of minutes." She pointed down a short hall. "Third door on the right."

The room was dark and quiet. Hal gave a quick, soft warning knock and then pushed the door open. I followed him inside and nearly ran into him as he stopped short.

"What's wrong?" I stepped around him and blinked in surprise. It took me a beat to figure out what I was seeing.

The hospital bedding was in disarray, pulled from the mattress on one side, and trailing down to the floor. It looked like Polly had slid out of bed and pulled the covers with her before untangling them from her legs and leaving them where they fell. The IV pole stood beside the bed, liquid dripping slowly from the needle onto the floor. The tape that had probably been holding the needle in Polly's arm had been flung on top of the sheets.

The closet near the bathroom was open. It was empty, a plastic hanger lying on the floor.

Polly was gone.

Hal turned on his heel and headed back out to the nurse's station.

Doc Janna was no longer there, but the nurse

she'd spoken to before was clearly surprised to hear that her patient wasn't in bed where she was supposed to be. She jumped up and hurried toward Polly's recovery room. A moment later, she ran back out and started to search, sending the other nurses scurrying to help.

Twenty minutes later, they had to accept the fact that Polly Doe had left the hospital. Mere hours from surgery and heavily medicated.

As Hal asked to watch the security tapes for the floor, I couldn't help wondering, what would scare the woman so badly that she would walk out of a hospital with a freshly repaired stab wound in her side.

Who was she running from?

And what had she done to become a target?

***

"There!" Hal said, jabbing a finger at the screen. "That's her."

"What's she doing?" I asked, leaning closer to the computer as the large woman with the wild tangle of blonde hair moved quickly down the hall, one hand covering the wound beneath her soiled clothes. As we watched, Polly stopped in front of a door and looked around before turning the knob and disappearing into it.

We watched several more moments but Polly

never came back out. The doc fast-forwarded another half hour, and we watched a tall man in scrubs step inside the room and then come out a couple of moments later. He headed across the hall, punched the button for the elevator, and then disappeared into it.

Hal turned to Doc Janna. "What is that room?"

The doc sighed. "A break room."

"Show us," Hal demanded, moving out from behind the nurse's station.

We all trailed the doc down the hallway, to an unmarked door across from the elevator. She turned the knob and sighed. "It's supposed to be locked." Shaking her head, she pushed it open.

The breakroom was more than just a spot to make coffee and toast a bagel. It was a large space, probably the size of three patient rooms, and there were two small couches in the center, with a couple of chairs to round out the lounging space. Closer to the door was a square table for eating and a short counter with a coffee maker and a microwave. A refrigerator filled the space between the end of the counter and the wall.

Privacy curtains on ceiling tracks, like those used in patient rooms, divided the back wall of the windowless space into three areas and separated them from the rest of the room. Hal walked over and tugged one of them back, revealing a large man sleeping on a bed.

It was the man we'd seen go into the room on the tape.

Hal looked at Doc Janna. "Do you, by any chance, store extra scrubs here?"

The doctor frowned, no doubt putting the pieces of the puzzle together along with us. "Yes. There's a closet full of them over there." She pointed toward a door on the sidewall near the back. Through the open door, I could see a restroom with a shower.

Hal sighed, shaking his head.

I felt his pain.

Polly Doe had evaded us again.

13

Caphy cocked her head at Hal, her adorable floppy ears dancing as she moved. Her beautiful green gaze was locked on the hunk of chicken between the Greek god's fingers, and her tail alternated between quivering with excitement and thumping loudly against the floor.

"Say please," Hal instructed the pibl.

I grinned around the lip of my wine glass, already knowing the outcome but wanting to enjoy the show none-the-less.

He was sitting on the floor with his back to the island, long legs stretched out in front of him and crossed at the ankles. Hal had been trying to get the pibl to beg for her food for several minutes with zero luck.

I could have told him.

Caphy would sing for her supper. And usually

did. Loudly. But she would not lower herself to doing any of the usual tricks humans taught a dog that wants food.

"She's not going to do it," I finally told Hal. I watched the cat jump effortlessly onto the countertop behind Hal, and my grin widened. The show was about to get even better.

He narrowed his gaze on me as if he thought I was being unnecessarily negative, and I twisted my lips to hide a smile.

"Come on, Caphy, girl. Say please." He barked to illustrate what he was looking for in the way of acquiescence, and Caphy cocked her head the other way, whining softly. She clearly thought he'd lost his mind.

Behind Hal, LaLee got into position, dropping soundlessly from the countertop to the tall stool mere inches from Hal's head.

Caphy's tail started to whip from side to side with excitement.

The game was afoot.

I gave in to the urge to grin.

Hal wouldn't even see it coming.

"Come on, girl, speak!"

LaLee slid her gaze to me and I thought I saw a sparkle there, almost buried behind the Siamese cat's usual arrogance.

I gave her a jaunty salute.

"Say plea..."

LaLee reached down and batted Hal on the head.

Hal jumped, glancing up. "Hey, pretty gir..."

Quick as a sneeze, the pibl snatched the treat from Hal's fingers.

"Hey!" Hal objected.

Bouncing happily, Caphy gave him a wet kiss right on the mouth.

He grimaced, drying his face with his sleeve. "Pibl cooties," he complained.

The cat jumped down and wound once around him, her tail a lazy salute in the air. Then she headed for me, knowing she'd be rewarded for her part in the Great Chicken Larceny.

I was laughing as I handed a bite of chicken down to her.

"You've been training them," Hal accused.

If only I was capable. The three fur-babies had formed themselves into a tiny, adorable little gang of food pick-pockets.

They worked together, and they were unstoppable.

Mostly because I always rewarded their thievery. They were just too cute to resist.

Still laughing, I decided I'd let him continue thinking I was the evil genius behind their little game. The truth was I'd been their first victim. And second. And third. And...

The small tent across the room twitched open, revealing a tiny, black and white pig, ears trembling and tail twirling happily behind her. She bounded over to Hal, apparently thrilled to see him sitting at her level, and burrowed into his middle, snuffling and snorting against him.

Hal laughed as Ethel affectionately headbutted him, and then reached behind him for the tiny stuffed pig which had been Ethel's last gift from her previous owner.

She grabbed the toy and bounced happily over to me, dropping it as I offered her a sweet, baby carrot from my salad bowl. "Here you go, pretty piggy."

The doorbell rang. I shoved to my feet. "I wonder who that is. Are you expecting Arno?" I asked my delicious but gullible PI.

"Not until later." Hal got to his feet before Ethel could return to headbutt him again and started clearing the table. "I'll put these in the dishwasher."

"Thank you," I said. Giving him a grateful smile, I headed for the front door, my three fur-babies trotting along with me.

Well, the pig and the cat were with me. Caphy was already trying to create a pibl-shaped hole in the door by flinging her almost seventy-pound self repeatedly against the wood.

"Hey, Caphy!" A familiar voice said through the door. Caphy lunged into new spasms of delight. She added pibl-fuel to her manic attack on the door as I tried to shove past her and unlock it.

I was already smiling when I opened the door. "Lis!"

My friend threw herself at me and then yelped as Caphy jumped up and swiped her arm with a wide, wet tongue.

I realized a moment later, as Caphy disappeared into the darkened yard that she was probably yelping over the pig snout in her belly rather than the Caphy kiss. "Ethel!" My BFF let go of me to bend over the little pot-bellied pig. "Joey, she's adorable!" Lis said.

It was the first time Lis had seen Ethel face-to-face. We'd only gotten her at Christmas time, and Lis hadn't been home since then.

Ethel Squeaks snorfled happily, smashing herself against Lis's leg and fixing her beadlike, black gaze on Lis' face as if she considered her a new best friend.

"She's so sweet," Lis said, running her hand over the soft, pink sweater Ethel was currently wearing. "How are they all getting along?"

"Too well," said a deep voice from the kitchen. We turned as Hal came out of the room, still drying his hands on a towel that was covered in tiny pigs. "They're a furry food gang now. Joey's training them to run scams."

Lis gave me a look of pure delight and I winked. "Come in," I said, looping my arm through hers. "It's been too long since we've seen you."

Hal grabbed the edge of the front door to push it closed but stopped at a muffled shout and a thump. He pulled it wide again, peering out onto the wide front porch. "Beware the dog," he said, grinning.

"Oh yeah," Lis said, grinning. "I ran into somebody outside."

"Apparently, so did Caphy," I mumbled.

Arno came limping in, Caphy shoving past him at the door and nearly knocking him to his fine backside again.

"That dog's a menace," he growled, earning a trio of laughs rather than the compassion he'd no doubt been hoping for.

"She's excited to see you," I told him. And Caphy's excited greetings often ended in somebody hitting the ground.

The aforementioned pibl and her porcine partner in crime took off running through the house together, nails and hooves clattering loudly on the wooden floor.

LaLee yowled at Lis, hissed, and then quickly rubbed her head against Lis's jeans-clad calf before heading upstairs to her favorite spot on my bed.

"Still a diva, I see."

I rolled my eyes. "You have no idea."

"Wine or beer?" Hal asked as we all headed into the kitchen.

"Beer*wine*," they said together, and then grinned at each other.

"Got it," Hal said. "Beer for the lady, wine for the gentleman."

Lis snorted, "Lady?"

I headed for the pantry. Despite having just had dinner, I grabbed a bag of chips and opened the fridge to pluck a container of dip from its depths. Having Lis show up felt like a party. And seeing the way she and Arno were looking at each other made me want to celebrate.

"You at least pretend to be a lady," I told her, sipping my own wine. "My cutoff jean shorts and flipflops pretty much scream bumpkin." I dumped the whole bag of chips into a large clear glass bowl.

Hal gave me a gentle kiss. "Lady isn't a fashion designation, honey. It's a state of mind." He snuck a chip from the bowl. "And you definitely qualify." He threw Lis a glance. "Both of you."

Arno nodded, tapping his wine against Lis' beer. "The man's not wrong."

I set the chips on the table and returned to the island to scoop the dip from the plastic tub into a smaller clear glass bowl. "Not that I'm complaining, girlfriend. But what are you doing here? Don't you have a shoot in Italy this month?"

Lis and Arno shared a look. I felt my eyes go wide, my mouth opening to take a leap. Fortunately, Lis stopped me from saying something that would have embarrassed us all.

"I'm not going on the shoot."

My eyes went wide. "Really? Why not?"

She set her beer down and took a chip. I was a little surprised to see her eating the fatty treat. She rarely ate empty calories for fear of gaining weight. "I..." She held the chip without biting into it, her gaze on the table.

My smile turned upside down. "Are you okay? Your mom?"

Lis looked up and laughed, tears brimming her beautiful eyes. "I'm fine. Mom's fine. I'm not going on the shoot because I quit."

Torn between relief and surprise, I just stared at her, unsure what to say.

"I took another job," she said.

"You did?" A wisp of excitement trilled through me. I was afraid to give in to it, but I had to ask. "Where? What job?"

Lis' beautiful face blossomed with pleasure. "Here in Deer Hollow. I'm going to work with Madge."

I squealed.

She laughed. "I'm going to train to be a realtor."

I squealed again and threw myself at her, pulling her from her chair. We danced around the kitchen together for a few beats, both of us crying.

Caphy ran into the kitchen, the pig at her heels, and the two of them followed us around the room, looking worried.

I finally let go of Lis and hugged my dog. "It's okay, sweet girl. Lis is moving home! Isn't that great?"

Caphy barked enthusiastically.

Hal quickly said, "Speak, Caphy."

I laughed. "Nice try, Amity."

14

"She's really been overwhelmed," Lis said, scooping up a generous amount of dip and taking a bite. Her eyes closed and a look of pure pleasure suffused her face. "Oh, dang. That's good." She opened her eyes again and grinned. "I might get fat."

She said it like it would be her new hobby. I laughed. "You've earned a few pounds."

She nodded. "I stopped by the office before I came here and spoke to Madge."

The fact that her smile was gone told me what they'd talked about. "She told you what's going on at the auction?"

Lis nodded, her expression earnest. "She feels really bad about the key, Joe."

I sighed. "I get it. She had no way of knowing that woman was up to no good."

"What *is* she up to anyway? And who is she? I've never met a Polly here in Deer Hollow," Lis said.

"I didn't recognize her either, but I think she might be several years older than we are."

Hal nodded. "I'm putting her at closer to thirty. Though, there's no reason to assume she's from Deer Hollow. She could have come from Indy for all we know."

And there it was. Everything always seemed to tie back to Indianapolis. I looked at Arno. "Are you looking into her background? Specifically, any ties to Garland Medford?"

"Not yet. As far as I can see she's clean."

"Any service record?"

Lis and I turned to Hal. His question seemed out of left field.

He noticed our surprise. "The person who was shooting at us knew his or her way around a rifle," Hal explained.

"I know I suggested it myself," I told him. "But I'm having trouble wrapping my mind around it. We know for a fact that she was attacked at the trailer. She's a victim in this, isn't she?" I said.

"Is she?" Arno asked, popping a chip into his mouth. He chewed and swallowed, grabbing his wine. "We don't know who she was fighting in that trailer. And why does she keep running? It makes her look like she has something to hide."

"Not to change the subject," Lis said. "But Madge

is worried because her client from Indy is really pressuring her to show him the auction," Lis said, staring at her beer bottle. "Is it possible he has something to do with this mess?"

"Very possible," Arno agreed. "We're doing background on him too."

We sat in silence for a few moments, each of us lost in our own thoughts. Hal finally glanced at Arno. "Did you get the DNA results on the blood in the car?"

Arno expelled air, "Yes, sorry. I can't believe I forgot to tell you. It was Lucklin's blood."

I frowned, trying to put the pieces together. "But I thought he was killed in the annex building."

"He was. There was too much blood there for him to have been killed somewhere else and then moved. But he did have a recently broken nose and a couple of facial contusions, which would explain the blood we found in the car."

"So he was beaten first, then killed," Hal said, nodding. "Seems he was having a very bad, horrible, rotten day."

We laughed.

"How did he get from the car to the annex?" I asked.

Lis glanced from one to the other of us, looking lost. "I have no idea what any of you are talking about."

"I'll fill you in later," Arno said with a smile.

I barely kept from wagging my eyebrows at that promise. There would be a "later"? That was good.

"Here's what I think happened," Arno said. "I think Lucky stole the money that fell out of the armored car and hid it. I'm guessing the thieves found out somehow that he had it and tried to beat the location of the money out of him. Maybe he buried it at Mitzner's, or maybe he just lied and said he did. Either way, they threw him into the trunk and took him to the garden store. Lucky must have escaped them at Mitzner's, and gone into hiding at the safest place he could think of."

"The auction," I said, nodding.

"Right. He'd know it was abandoned, and there was no trail leading to him there."

"But he couldn't show his face, so he had Polly get the key for him," Hal added.

"Right," Arno agreed.

"What about the car?" I asked. "Why'd they leave it at Mitzner's?"

"It's stolen," Arno said. He took a sip of his wine. "They had to dump it somewhere."

"But Joey and Hal were just attacked," Lis said, looking confused. "Somebody's still not happy."

"True," Arno said. "That's an open switch in this mess. Hopefully, Polly will be able to fill in some of the blanks when we find her."

"If she's still alive," Arno said.

I grimaced.

"Have you processed the trailer yet?" Hal asked.

"Yes. Fingerprints from Lucklin, Polly, and of course, his mom."

I lifted my brows. "His mom was there?"

Arno nodded. "From my discussion with her, she apparently cleaned it for him."

I shook my head. "I guess some men never grow up."

Lis snorted.

"When we spoke to her, Angie Lucklin didn't admit to knowing about the trailer," Hal said. "She gave us the address for an apartment in Indy."

"Really?" Arno asked, intrigued. "That's interesting. "

"Yeah, isn't it?" Hal agreed. "Maybe we need to talk to Lucky's mom again."

"If Angie was at the trailer, I'll bet she knows Polly too. Maybe she can tell us more about her," I said.

Arno's cell phone rang. He glanced at the name on the screen and stood. "Excuse me. I need to take this."

He headed outside.

I glanced at Lis. "So, are you going to live with your mom?"

"Ha! Not a chance. Madge said Penney's place is still available."

My eyes went wide. "Ooooh! That's a really pretty house. You'll love it."

"You've been there?"

Hal snorted, "LaLee's former home? Yeah. The memory is forever etched in my arms."

When Lis narrowed her gaze at him, I explained. "LaLee wasn't a fan of being put into her cat carrier. She got kind of..."

"Catty?" Hal supplied helpfully.

Lis and I laughed.

Arno's footsteps in my foyer were heavy and fast. Our heads swiveled to the door as he came inside. "I have to go. That was Deputy Schmidt. They found a body at Mitzner's."

It was dark and cold. The moon was fat in an iron-gray sky. Slender ribbons of clouds skimmed quickly past overhead, creating shadows that temporarily blocked the moon's silver light.

The air was rich with freshly turned soil. Spicy with the pungent tang of fresh manure. Hal parked the Escalade near the entrance, well behind the two Sheriff's vehicles parked further in, near a small building that I remembered was generally filled with hanging plants.

Lis rubbed her arms, her stylish denim jacket no match for the cooler night temps.

I dug into the back of the SUV and pulled out a blanket, handing it to her.

"Thanks." Wrapping it around her shoulders, she sneezed, giving the blanket a quick sniff. "Is this Caphy's blanket?"

I pretended I hadn't heard the question and hurried after Hal. The truth was even worse than my BFF suspected. It was our picnic blanket. But I hadn't washed it since Caphy and Ethel had shared it the last time we'd gone to the park.

I grinned as Lis sneezed again. With her long strides, she quickly caught up to me and looped her arm through mine. "You rat. The pig used this for a wallow, didn't she?"

I snorted out a laugh. "She didn't wallow, exactly. But she and Caphy had a nice roll on it the last time it was out."

She sighed. "You and your critters."

Yeah. Me and my critters.

We walked for a really long time, heading toward what had to be the very back of Mitzner's property and a battered old wood building tucked behind a copse of large evergreens.

Hal turned to us as we approached the building. "Stay back, so you don't contaminate the scene."

I barely kept from sticking my tongue out at him. "Contaminate? Us?" I murmured.

Lis squeezed my arm. "Come on. There's probably a side entrance or a window. If we're lucky, we can get a line of sight on the body."

"I like how you think," I told her.

We walked around the building, staying a few feet away from the wall just to make sure we didn't tromp on anything important.

On the long side facing the evergreens, there was a spot where a couple of boards had broken or been pushed out. Fortunately, there were no cops there to stop us from huddling against the wall and peering inside.

Lis sucked in a gasp when we saw the body.

I grimaced.

Hal's gaze skimmed in our direction but he didn't give us away.

"Well, that's certainly unique," I said.

The dead man was hanging from the uplifted forks of a forklift, one arm looped over each fork, and a rope looped around his throat to keep him from falling all the way through. Upon closer inspection, I saw that his arms were tied too. He'd probably been tied to the machine on the ground, and then the fork was lifted until the rope around his throat did its gruesome job.

"Somebody meant business," Lis murmured.

She wasn't wrong. The sight in the old building caused ice to form in my belly. That kind of brutality was the trademark of a certain gangster from Indianapolis. One who meant my family harm.

I didn't think the current mess had anything to do with my mother. Not directly. But I was sure that Garland Medford would recognize an opportunity to scare her when he saw it.

I shuddered.

Lis opened the blanket and drew me into it with her.

Hal came over a moment later, speaking to us through the hole in the wall. "Guy has an Indy license," he told us. "It's probably a good guess that he was the driver of the abandoned rental car."

"How long has he been there?" I asked.

"A couple of days. Buck only found him a couple of hours ago. He apparently hasn't been using this building, except for storage. Unfortunately, Arno's deputy missed it because it was hidden behind those trees."

"How did he die?" I asked, though I thought I had a good idea.

"Asphyxiation," Hal confirmed. "I'm going to do background on this guy tonight, honey. If he's tied to Medford, I'll find out."

I nodded.

"Garland Medford?" Lis asked, her eyes wide. "You think he's involved in this?"

Hal shrugged. "We need to make sure he's not. Besides, there are too many strings tying this back to Indy for my comfort."

I bit my bottom lip. My thoughts exactly.

"Hopefully not," Hal added, reaching out to squeeze my arm. "Why don't you two wait in the car, where it's warmer?"

I shook my head. "I want to stay here."

He sighed and returned to the body.

Schmidt was circling the man, taking pictures. If I closed my eyes, the constant snap and flash of the camera would have sounded like a photoshoot. I'd gone to a few of Lis's shoots in the early days, thinking like she had that the whole modeling thing was fun and glamorous.

But there was nothing fun or glamorous about the corpse hanging from the forklift.

I forced my emotions back and tried to view the scene with an analytical eye.

He was a medium-sized guy. Probably about five feet ten inches tall. His dark brown hair was cut short on the sides and back and longer on the top. He wore a blue suit, the color too bright to be conservative, and the pinstriped shirt was unbuttoned at his throat. There was no tie.

His shoes didn't match the suit. In fact, they weren't shoes at all. They were more like hiking boots, with oversized tread.

My mind spun me back to the scene of Lucky's murder. Where there had been two sets of tracks in the dust...

I swallowed hard.

The dead man's head hung to his chest. I could

see a large purple knot on his temple, and I surmised he'd been knocked out before being tied to the machine. For his sake, I hoped he'd stayed that way.

The building was full of gardening supplies. Large rectangles of peat moss and bags of manure were piled along the walls. A pile of loose black soil dominated the front corner of the building. The forklift had driven through the soil, spreading it around the space, its tracks pressing the scattered black dirt into the clay floor.

On the floor next to the forklift, a pair of what looked like expensive sunglasses lay bent and filthy.

"His knuckles are bruised and bloody," Lis muttered softly.

I looked at the dead guy's hand, hanging limply at about shoulder level. She was right. He'd been in a fight sometime before he was killed.

It seemed very likely that he'd beaten a certain Lance Lucklin and broken his nose.

15

Hal dropped Lis and me off at my house and left, making me promise to put on the alarm and call him if I heard anything that sounded wrong.

Anything at all.

I hadn't been too worried until he'd given me that instruction, adding a stern, worried countenance to the mix.

"I'll be fine," I told him. "I have LaLee to protect me."

Lis snorted. "I noticed you didn't propose the pittbrat could save you."

I grinned. Caphy had actually saved my life once. She'd taken a bullet that had been meant for me. I would never forget how horrible that night had been. But I was realistic about the pibl. Most of the time, she was more likely to beat an intruder to death with her muscular, wagging tail than bite him.

As Hal maneuvered the big car down my long, winding drive, Lis glanced my way. "I can stay."

I shook my head. "It's not necessary. Hal's just being a worry-wart. This mess has nothing to do with me." Even as I said the words, I hoped they were true. "You go on home and tell your mom the good news. She's going to be so excited."

Lis' gorgeous face lit up with a smile. "She's going to pee herself. She's been trying to get me to move home for years. We'll talk tomorrow?"

I nodded, waving as she climbed into her cute little sports car and followed Hal out to the road.

I expelled a breath, breathing deeply of the cool night air and feeling some of the tightness in my muscles relaxing. It was so quiet in the country at night. The sky had cleared, and millions of silvery points of light filled the sky. Despite the cold that continued to cling to the rolling, green land around Deer Hollow most days, I could smell Spring in the air.

I stood there another minute, trying to ignore the pitty's frantic warbling and the sound of her furry body slamming against the front door. When I couldn't take it anymore, I let Caphy out to do her thing. She'd make her final circuit of the property, and then she'd settle down for the night in her favorite spot.

Draped over my lower legs in an unmovable sprawl.

As I watched the pibl bounce around the yard, Ethel Squeaks wandered out and gave me a smushy head-butt. "Hey, pretty piggy." With a spin of her adorable tail, the pig wandered out to the yard and joined her best friend in a carefree security circuit of the yard.

I'd locked up, put the alarm on, and was heading into the bathroom to wash my face and brush my teeth when Caphy's head jerked up. She went unnaturally still, her green eyes dark pools of intensity in the low light.

I stilled too, every nerve in my body pinging an alert.

LaLee stood up and stretched, arching her back as she yawned. I would have felt better if she'd have lain back down and gone back to sleep. But she sat in the middle of the bed, eyes riveted on the bay window that overlooked the front yard. The fur on her long back stood at attention.

Not good.

Caphy growled low in her throat and, as I stepped away from the window, she jumped down from the bed and leaped onto the cushioned seat, ears flat and tail rigid with alarm.

"What is it, girl?" I asked softly. My heart banged

against my ribs. My face felt tight and hot. Alarm had me firmly in its grip.

Caphy lunged at the window, snarling. The violence of her movement spurred me to action.

I turned and ran toward the bathroom, where I thought I'd left my phone.

It wasn't there.

It took me a beat to realize I'd left it in the kitchen.

Dangit!

Did I want to go down there and get it?

The doorbell rang and I jumped, collapsing back against the counter and placing a hand over my heart as if to stop it from trying to explode through my ribs.

I laughed at myself.

Killers probably didn't ring the doorbell. I was pretty sure that stealth was a key component of their job description.

I grabbed an oversized black sweatshirt that had a colorful depiction of a Pitbull on the front, and dragged it over my head to cover my tank top and braless state.

The boxers I generally wore to sleep in would be fine to answer the door in.

As I opened the bedroom door, the doorbell sounded again. Caphy lunged past me, nearly knocking me over in a mad dash to get to the door.

I heard Ethel's hooves clicking over the tiles of the foyer as I started down the stairs.

LaLee brushed past me in the dark, her fur warm and silky against my skin.

Feeling jittery and unsettled, I diverted to the kitchen and grabbed my phone, texting Hal before heading toward the door. I leaned my ear against it. "Who's there?"

"Miss Fulle?"

I frowned at the deep, cultured tone of the voice, not recognizing it. "Please tell me who you are."

After a slight hesitation, he said, "I'm a friend of your mother's."

Panic flared through me. Stars burst before my gaze. With a terrifying jolt, I knew who it was.

I shouldn't open the door. Especially with Caphy still growling softly against my thigh. But rage ate through the last of my reluctance. I grabbed the handle, unlocked the deadbolt, and yanked the door open before I could stop myself.

I'd seen pictures of him in the papers and once in a business magazine. The photos had been moments captured in time, perfect depictions of a wealthy, self-assured man doing what he did best... charming people to get what he wanted.

They hadn't done him justice.

I thought he was in his late forties. Young for a man who'd taken the business world by storm and built both a fortune and an empire within a handful of years. Staring at him standing on my porch, his wary gaze fixed on my dog and his hands lifted, palms out as if in surrender, I could almost see the charm that pulled others into his sphere and held them there.

Though not as tall as Hal, he looked to be a couple of inches over six feet. His mahogany-brown hair was long, thick and wavy, tucked behind his ears and curling softly at the back of his strong neck. He wore a starched white shirt, open at the throat and sleeves rolled to show strong, tanned forearms. His charcoal slacks were creased with precision. His loafers appeared expensive.

When he smiled, strong white teeth flashed in a mouth that was wide and attractively formed.

He was almost too perfect.

"What do you want?" I asked Garland Medford.

Rather than seeming to be offended by my tone, the man who'd probably ordered the murder of my father smiled wider. He looked pleased by my anger.

"Miss Fulle. You're even more beautiful than I expected." He cocked his head, his charcoal gaze sliding over my bare legs. "The spitting image of your mother."

Rage made my lungs tighten, and I suddenly found it hard to draw a breath. "Don't ever speak of my mother. Or anyone I know or love."

The smile flattened out, and the gaze softened. "Joey, you have the wrong idea..."

I clenched my fists and took a step toward him, fully intending to pop him in the face.

Caphy's growl turned to a snarl. She lunged at him, teeth bared and spittle flying. I barely managed to grab hold of her collar, protecting her rather than him.

A man like Medford wouldn't have come to my house unarmed or unprepared. He had too many skeletons in the closet to assume that any transaction would be safe. Especially one where he surprised the supposedly lone survivor of a family he'd destroyed.

A car door opened behind Medford and I was glad I'd stopped Caphy from taking a chunk out of him as a man climbed out of the big car, one hand sliding beneath his suit coat for the weapon he no doubt had holstered there. "Are you all right, Mr. Medford?" the thug asked.

Medford lifted a hand and half turned. "We're fine, Tulliver. No worries."

"You're not fine," I told him, loud enough for his thug to hear. "You're far from fine. Now get off my property before I forget I care about going to prison and kill you myself."

Medford narrowed his gaze on me, clearly taking my measure. Finally, he sighed, his expression sad. "You've got me all wrong, Miss Fulle. I had nothing to do with your parents' death..." He arched a perfectly shaped brow when rage filled my face with heat and color. "But I see you don't believe me. I'm actually not here about that. I came to tell you that I had nothing to do with the fire and the shooting at your place."

His denial surprised me. "Tell that to the police."

He chuckled without mirth. "I will. But I wanted you to know it too. I had nothing to do with the armored truck robberies. Those weren't my people. And it isn't my people who are trying to get the money back now."

Lights blossomed at the end of my drive, and a large engine roared as the car sped toward the house.

Hal.

A soft warmth played over my calves. I looked down in horror as LaLee trotted out onto the porch, long tail whipping.

"No, LaLee!" I tried to grab her, afraid she'd take off into the dark and Hal and I would have to chase her down before the coyotes found her.

But the Siamese cat wasn't interested in running off. Instead, she trotted over to Medford, offering him a deep-throated yowl and rubbing against his perfectly pressed slacks.

I stood there in shock, hoping she left a lot of hair behind on those slacks.

"What a pretty kitty," Medford said, reaching down to scratch her between her pert, mahogany-colored ears.

Like an unstable shapeshifter, LaLee turned from sweet pet to enraged demon in the blink of an eye. Hissing like she meant it, she sank her fangs into Medford's hand and followed it up with a swipe of her razor-sharp claws.

"Ow!" Medford yanked his hand back and formed it into a fist, rage darkening his too-handsome face.

LaLee couldn't have cared less. With a final switch of her expressive tail, the Siamese spitfire spun around and trotted back past me into the house.

"What's going on?" Hal asked, his hand resting on the gun at his back.

Medford pulled a pristine hanky out of his pocket and mopped at the blood beading up on his hand, eyeing me.

I smiled meanly. "Just introducing Garland Medford to LaLee and Caphy," I told the Greek god.

And, right on cue, Caphy snarled and lunged.

16

I barely caught her in time. My fingers curled tightly around Caphy's collar as she lunged, spittle flying at the gangster holding a gun on her.

Behind him, I heard a thud and the ratcheting of a 9-millimeter. I was afraid to move and couldn't look away from Medford and the gun he had pointed at my dog.

"Put it away, Medford," said a deep, dangerous voice about five feet behind the gangster.

Other than a slight widening of his eyes, Medford didn't react to the fact that Hal had so easily incapacitated his thug.

"I'm just trying to protect myself," Medford said, his gun-hand steady.

Doing a decent job of mirroring my unhappy dog, I curled my lips away from my teeth. "If you shoot my dog, there won't be anything that will protect you, Medford."

I was shaking from rage, but I tried to clamp down on it because I was sure the gangster would interpret it as fear.

I was afraid. But not for myself. If he hurt Caphy...

Medford finally lowered the gun.

Hal took two long strides and settled his gun into Medford's back. Reaching around the man in front of me, Hal relieved him of his gun too. "What are you doing here?" he asked my unwelcome visitor.

Medford gave me a cool, unconcerned smile. "I just wanted to warn Joey about what she was dealing with."

"Isn't that just so kind of you," I said sarcastically. I tugged Caphy back and shoved her into the house, closing the door in her worried face. "Especially since you had my parents killed." I felt my lips curling again and fought to get control. "It would have been nice if you'd considered my welfare before you did that."

Medford shook his head. "I didn't kill your parents..." he started to say. Something in my gaze stopped him. He sighed. "But you aren't going to believe that, are you?"

"No," I answered. Brief and uncompromising.

"I think it's time for you to go, Medford," Hal told him.

Medford half-turned, glancing at his unconscious bodyguard on the driveway. "How do you propose I do that since you've incapacitated my driver?"

"Here's a wild thought," Hal said. "Drive yourself."

Medford sighed. He started down the steps, his movements unhurried and his demeanor unconcerned. At the car, a silver Lexus, he kicked the unconscious driver in the hip, just hard enough to jolt the man awake. "Get in the car. I'm driving," he told his guard in a voice that didn't bode well for the man's future employment.

As his thug stumbled around to the passenger side door, Medford turned back to me. "You don't believe me. I know that. But some of the things you've been led to believe about me aren't true. Some of the people who've...hurt...you have had motives they didn't get from me." He pulled the car door open. "This thing with the stolen money, it has nothing to do with me, and, although it has nothing to do with you either, you *will* be in danger if you pursue it." When Hal tensed at what sounded too much like a threat, Medford shook his head. "Not a threat, Amity. Just the facts."

He started to climb into the Lexus and stopped, turning back to me with a neutral expression that wasn't at all threatening or angry. "Please give my regards to your mother."

My heart stopped beating. My lungs ceased to draw air. I stumbled backward until I came up against the front door and couldn't go any further. I slumped against the cool wood, trying to breathe around the panic turning my body to stone.

I was vaguely aware of the car pulling away.

A deep voice came to me from the end of a long, long tunnel. A concerned voice.

Warm, supportive arms wrapped me in an embrace that should have filled me with comfort.

But they didn't. There was no comfort to be had. In a fog, my lips repeating a single word—*no, no, no, no, no, no, no*—I felt my sanity melting away from me in a violent wash of pure terror.

"Breathe, Joey!" Hal demanded, his hands firm to the point of pain on my arms.

Suddenly, he scooped me up and shoved the door open behind me, carrying me into the house and settling me on the couch. His hands gently slapped my face.

The couch cushion dented beneath me, and a soft tongue bathed my hands. A warm weight dropped alongside my hip.

Slowly, I felt the world returning around me.

I inhaled deeply, filling my chest with much-needed air. The stars that had been spinning franti-cally before my eyes burst and fell away, and the terror brought me upright on the couch. My hand snapped out to clutch Hal's wrist in what had to be a painful grip. My nails dug into his skin, and I had to make a conscious effort to unclench my fingers. "We have to warn her," I told him, my gaze a frantic plea locked on his face.

He nodded. "We will, honey. But if Medford could get to her, he already would have."

My head was shaking. "He was telling me that he was going after her."

"He's playing mind games," Hal told me, his big, warm hand cupping my face. I shivered violently, my cheek burrowing into the warmth of that hand as if I'd die without it.

Maybe I would.

I dug my fingers into Caphy's fur and scratched, the motion an instinctual attempt to regain my moorings.

"We need to tell her," I said again. "She needs to know she's exposed."

Hal opened his mouth as if to argue and then closed it, nodding. "I'll call Arno. He has Devon's number."

Though I had always called him Uncle Dev, Devon Little wasn't really my uncle. When my dad had been killed, Dev had taken it upon himself to keep my mom and me safe. Mostly that meant keeping my mom away from me since they were pretty sure Medford would leave me alone if my parents were presumed dead.

A thought dug its way up from the murky wash

of fear clogging my senses. I jerked my gaze to Hal's. "Edward Johnston! That's who he was talking about."

Johnston had been involved in some pretty ugly stuff a few months earlier and had managed to get out of Deer Hollow before he could be arrested, leaving his wife to take the fall for their illegal shenanigans.

"He still has a score to settle with us," I said. If it weren't for Hal and me, he wouldn't have had to run.

"It's possible it's him," Hal agreed. He stood. "I'm going to make you some hot tea."

I nodded, settling back against the couch to think. "Thanks," I said, almost absently.

If Johnston was back, I was indeed in danger. But I had no idea how Polly and Lucky were involved. Had they been working for Johnston? And, if so, what had they done to earn a spot on his "To be Killed" list?

I heard Hal's voice and realized he was talking on his phone. I got up and headed for the kitchen, Caphy trotting along behind me.

Ethel was snarfing up some berries from a small bowl when we came into the kitchen. Hal showed me a second bowl and nodded toward Caphy. He was a smart man and knew that, if Caphy didn't have her own snack, she'd soon be stealing Ethel's.

I grabbed Caphy's collar when she started toward

the pig and took the bowl with my other hand. Then I enticed the pitty toward the mudroom with the snack and closed the door to keep her there.

I got myself a glass of water, feeling drained from my emotional tsunami.

"Yeah, she's right here. I'll tell her. Thanks, Arno."

He disconnected.

"Tell me what?" I asked.

"He texted Devon while we were on the phone and they're fine."

I sighed, relief taking the last of the starch from my limbs. "Thank heaven."

He slid his arms around my waist and pulled me close. I closed my eyes and let his warmth and delicious male scent wash over me. We stood that way for a long moment, only the sound of Ethel's snorfling and Caphy's whining behind the door filling the silence.

A moment later, the soft sound of Ethel's hooves on the hard floor and the bump of her snout against my leg had my eyes snapping open. I looked down at her, noting the worried glint in her shiny pebble eyes and the tentative twitch of her ears. "I'm okay, sweet girl," I told her, letting go of Hal to give the pig a hug.

She trotted away for a beat and came back with her yellow ball, dropping it at my feet.

I grinned. "Thank you, Miss Squeaks. That's such a nice gift."

She tapped the ball with her snout.

Hal chuckled softly. "She wants you to throw it."

Of course she did. I threw the ball into the hallway and she trotted after it, squealing softly with pleasure.

Caphy's whining rose a notch. The door rumbled under her determined scratching.

Hal let her out of the mudroom, and she took off in the direction Ethel had gone.

I smiled, knowing they'd entertain themselves for the next few minutes with the ball.

"She thought playing with the ball would make you feel better," Hal told me with a fond smile.

I laughed. "She was half right. Watching *them* play with it definitely does."

"You want something to eat?" Hal asked me.

I shook my head. "I'm not hungry, thanks."

He nodded. "According to my research so far, the dead guy has second-hand ties to Garland. Bob Hadley?" he said to remind me.

I nodded.

"Hadley worked for him for a few years as a bodyguard. But they severed their relationship two months ago. Interestingly enough, that's about the time the armored car robberies started happening."

"So, no direct ties to him," I said, frowning.

"Medford skates again." Even to me, my voice sounded discouraged.

"You should get to bed," Hal said. "I'll sleep on the couch."

"You don't need to do that," I told him, knowing I didn't mean the words even as they left my mouth.

"Yes, I do. And I don't want to hear any argument. I was going to work much of the night anyway, and I can do that here as well as at my house."

I opened my mouth to try again but he covered my lips with a strong, warm finger. "I'm staying. I'll feel better."

I gave up, nodding. Tugging his finger away, I stretched up and placed my lips over his, letting my appreciation show in a lingering kiss. "I'll see you in the morning."

"You will."

I started up the stairs as the pig and the pitty rounded the stairwell in a full-out gallop toward Hal, who was making himself comfortable on the couch. His laptop was lying on the coffee table. I wondered when he'd brought that inside.

Shaking my head, I realized I'd been so wrapped up in my fear he could have walked right past me after Medford left and I wouldn't have noticed.

I was a mess.

The realization made me glad Hal had insisted on staying. I felt safe with him there. With that comforting thought, I headed up and climbed into my bed, shivering against the cool sheets.

With a soft meow, LaLee jumped onto the bed and snuggled close, purring loudly against the arm I draped around her.

I never knew when Caphy came up to join me. I was already dead to the world.

17

Angie Lucklin didn't look happy to see us. I knew the feeling. I wasn't happy to see her either. She'd most likely lied to us about her son's residence in Deer Hollow. That lack of information could have been dangerous. As it was, it had cost nothing more than a few mosquito bites and, in my case, mud in places I wasn't entirely sure I'd completely expunged.

I knocked on Angie's front door and looked around as we waited for her to answer. Through the woods behind her house, I could hear the familiar sound of the river roaring between its banks from a Spring downpour in the wee hours of the morning.

Hal hung back, examining something on the porch until he heard the door open. I didn't get the chance to ask what he was looking at before Angie was staring at us through the streaked glass of the screen door, her hands tugging on the sleeves of her long-sleeved tee-shirt.

Hal's face was less friendly than the last time we'd been there, his manner brusque. "We'd like to ask you a few more questions about your son."

She spun a worried gaze toward me and seemed to be considering closing the door in our faces. But she finally nodded and stepped forward, opening the door. "Come in. Can I get you some...?"

"No, thank you," Hal interrupted, making it clear we weren't there for a social call. He stopped just inside the door and held up his phone, showing her the photo of the ruined trailer home he'd taken when we'd arrived at Lucky's. "This is what's left of your son's hidey-hole by the river." He slid his finger over the screen and a second photo shifted into place. A stark, bloody handprint stood out against the pale metal of the damaged door.

Angie's gaze narrowed on the photos but she didn't break down, surprising me. I'd expected her to become remorseful about lying to us. I'd expected her to give us a tearful apology and follow that with an explanation we might or might not believe. Instead, she lifted a cold gaze to Hal, her thin lips curving in a slight, unhappy smile. "So what? Lance is dead. He doesn't need that trailer anymore."

"His girlfriend Polly needed it. But then someone attacked her, cut her up, and now she needs more than a place to live."

I had to admire Hal's artful delivery of facts, giving the woman just enough to make it sound as if Polly were a complete victim.

Angie tugged her long sleeves down over her wrists, lips pursing stubbornly. "I don't know anything about that."

"You don't know Polly?"

I found it interesting that Hal was focusing on that line of questioning. It wouldn't have been the way I'd have gone.

Angie shrugged. "The boy hooked up with girls now and then. He was male. As you know, they do that, Mr. Amity. It wasn't my business and I stayed out of it."

"Mrs. Lucklin, why didn't you tell us about the trailer when we were here before?"

She held his gaze without apparent fear. "I don't know you people from Adam," she said, belligerent. "I don't tell strangers my business. Besides, that trailer's been in our family for a couple of decades. If the boy chooses to use it once in a while, there's nothing odd in that."

I was shocked by her manner. She'd been so warm and friendly before. What had happened to create the wall of hostility against us?

"Deputy Willager explained to us that you cleaned the place for Lucky?"

Angie shrugged, but her gaze had gone shrewd. Had she thought we were lying about working with

Arno? "Once in a while."

"Mrs. Lucklin," I said gently. "We really are trying to find the person who killed your son. We're trying to help."

Angie blinked rapidly, her gaze going shiny with tears she refused to shed. Instead, she sniffed loudly and raised her chin. "If I knew who it was, I'd tell you. I don't."

"Did your son seem worried before he died? Did he mention anyone who was bothering him?" I asked.

Angie shook her head, her manner softening.

"Did he tell you about the money he found?" Hal asked gently.

Her gaze flashed to Hal. "Money? No. What money?"

It would have been hard to miss the sharpness in her questions. Either she was surprised to hear Lucky had found some money, or she was surprised that we knew about it.

"We believe he took money from the wrong person," Hal said. "We think that person is still looking for it. If you or Polly know where it is..."

Angie flinched. "Polly? How would I know if she has the money? I don't even know the girl."

"That might have been true before," Hal said. "But I don't think it is now. Is it Polly?"

He raised his voice on the last part, and I blinked in surprise.

Especially when a large blonde woman stepped around the door from the kitchen, one arm pressed against her belly.

Her shirt was still torn from the knife attack, the bandaging beneath it sported a bright bloom of blood. She glared at Hal. "How'd you know I was here?"

Hal jerked his head toward the porch. "Blood on the railing out there. You shouldn't have left the hospital early."

Polly winced as she moved to lean against the wall. "I had to. I wasn't safe there."

"Tell us who's after you, Polly," I said, happy to hear that my voice was steady. I'd been as surprised as Mrs. Lucklin by Hal's discovery.

She shook her head, frowning. "Who are you people?"

"I'm a private investigator working with the police. Joey's a citizen consultant."

I almost grinned. My only value to Hal was my knowledge of Deer Hollow and its people. But I guessed that was value enough, given that I was too nosy to stay out of the Sheriff's business. At least, this way, Arno didn't constantly have to yell at me to mind my own business.

I inclined my head to Polly. "I'm Joey Fulle. I'm afraid I don't know you, do I? I know most of the people in Deer Hollow." I smiled. "You know how it is? Small town," I said by way of explanation.

She snorted out a laugh, but it was edged with pain. "I'm from Ormsville. But Lucky and I met in Indianapolis." She winced, shifting her body as if she were in great pain. "I don't know who attacked me. The guy was wearing something over his face. He came out of nowhere. I was just making myself a snack and the door suddenly crashed open. He jumped on me before I could react."

"Did he ask you about the money?" Hal questioned.

Her gaze skimmed away. "There was no conversation."

Her response was too evasive for my taste. "He just started slashing at you?"

She chewed her lip. "Actually, I was the one who grabbed the knife off the counter. He got it away from me, and I ended up on the wrong end of it."

That was interesting.

"Did you manage to injure him with the knife before he took it," Hal asked, his expression gaining interest.

She shrugged. "I fought him off, earning a few nicks from the knife, but then he trapped me." A look of pride filled her round face. "He was expecting me to cower, but I charged him instead. That's where I got this." She looked down at her bandaged stomach. "It was like swallowing fire. But I shoved him back, and he hit his head on the cabinet and went down. I ran. When I got outside, I realized I had no car..."

"Did your attacker have a vehicle?"

She frowned as if it hadn't occurred to her. "No. Now that you mention it, he didn't. That's strange, isn't it?"

"Go on," Hal urged. "What happened then?"

"I realized there was no way I'd make it on foot, even if I went through the woods. So I got in that old boat and lay down on the bottom."

"You just let the currents take you," Hal supplied.

Polly nodded. "When the boat stuck on the sand, I climbed out and made my way through the woods. I saw that house and thought it would be a good place to rest." She scowled at Hal and me. "I woke up in the hospital. I'm guessing I have you two to thank for that?"

"You were in danger of bleeding to death," Hal said, unapologetic.

Polly's glare slid away.

"Did you help Lucky steal that money?" Hal asked.

As far as I knew, Pru hadn't told Hal there was more than one person involved in the money grab at the casino. Was Hal just guessing?

"He didn't steal anything. That money just fell in front of him. Anybody would have done what he did."

"Not likely," I murmured too low for the other

woman to hear. But Angie heard and her gaze sharpened on me.

"Were you with him?" Hal prompted again.

"No. When he came home he was wasted. He showed me the money and then passed out. I knew there were going to be repercussions for him grabbing the money, so I came up with a plan."

"Tell me about the plan," Hal urged.

Polly's face had turned ashen. With a soft groan, she bent over the arm that was braced against her side. I realized what it was taking out of her to stand there. But she firmed her jaw. "We...acquired a car and drove down here. I knew his mom lived in this little dustbowl of a town. I figured we'd be safe here."

"Acquired?" Hal asked.

Polly shrugged. "I don't know where Lucky got it." She skimmed a look at Hal from under her lashes, clearly not telling the truth.

"You came to Deer Hollow because you thought it would be safe. Did you think someone was coming after you?" Hal asked, not unkindly.

"We didn't think so at the time. We were just being careful. Lucky was good like that. We found out later they'd put a tracker in the bag. Somebody wasn't very trustworthy." She grinned, her lips pale from blood loss.

"The big sedan was yours? The one at Mitzner's?"

She nodded. "Lucky left me at the trailer, promising to come right back after he hid the money."

"Do you know where he hid it?"

She gave Hal a sly look. "No."

I didn't believe her. I could tell by the way his jaw tightened that Hal didn't either.

"Then what happened?"

She shrugged. "No idea. It all went wrong somehow. Next thing I know, Lucky's callin' to tell me to meet him at that auction place with a key. I'm yellin' at him that I had no idea how to get a key but he's insisting, telling me we had to use a key so nobody knew it had been broken into."

"You went to Deer Hollow Realtor," I said.

"Turned out, getting that key was easier than I thought it would be. I met him at the place and gave him the key. He told me to go back to the trailer and he'd be in touch."

"Did he have the money with him?"

"I don't know. He wasn't holding the bag, and he didn't have the car. When I asked him where it was, he just shook his head and told me not to worry about it. He knew what he was doin'." She grimaced in pain, her hand pressing against the bandage.

I noticed the blood shadow on the bandage had grown.

"He must have run into trouble," Polly said, her voice strained. "But he wouldn't tell me what happened." She grimaced. "He had a black eye. His nose was purple and kind of bent."

"How'd you get into town and then back to the auction?" Hal asked. "Deer Hollow's a good three miles up the highway from here, and it's a couple more to the auction."

"I..." She gasped, her face turning white.

I watched in shock as she slid down the wall, her eyes rolling back in her head as she passed out.

"Call an ambulance," Hal said as he hurried over and grabbed her before she toppled sideways and smacked her head against the hard-oak floor.

18

While we waited for the ambulance, Hal quizzed a reluctant Angie about Polly.

"Why'd you lie to us about knowing her?" he asked the older woman.

"I didn't lie. I just met her today. She begged me not to tell you she was here."

"Why's she running?"

"I'm not sure. But I got the feeling she thought the man who cut her up wasn't going to go away. I tried to get her to hand the money over. I told her it wasn't worth dying over. But she insists she doesn't know where it is."

"You believe her?"

Angie shrugged, rubbing her arms as if she were cold.

"Why'd she come to you?" Hal asked gently.

"She said Lance told her to come if she got into

trouble. He said I'd give her a place to hide out." Tears filled her eyes, and she scrubbed at them with the back of her hand. Her sleeve slid up at the motion and I spotted a smear of Polly's blood staining the skin of her thin arm. "You tried to help her," I said. It wasn't a question.

Angie didn't bother trying to stop the tears. She fell into a chair and stared down at her fisted hands. "I wanted to do it for Lance. He cared for the girl. It was the only thing I could do for him." She broke down into quiet sobs.

In the distance, sirens wailed toward us, growing rapidly closer.

"I'll go and show them in," I told Hal, relieved to escape from Angie Lucklin's obvious pain.

We watched the ambulance drive away with Polly, sirens and lights blazing, before returning to Hal's car. Climbing inside, we sat in silence for a long moment, both of us lost in our thoughts.

I was still trying to reconcile Garland Medford's arrival in my life, as well as his assertion that he had nothing to do with what was going on. Of course, I would expect him to deny his involvement. That wasn't a surprise. What did surprise me was that he'd knocked on my door just to tell me he wasn't involved.

Why had he come to Deer Hollow? He had no reason at all to tell me he was innocent. As far as I knew, nobody had been harassing him about my parents' accident.

Not recently, anyway.

To everyone but me, that was old news.

So why was he in Deer Hollow? What had he hoped to accomplish? Had he just wanted to scare me? Was he trying to flush out my mom?

Or had he been trying to warn me that Edward Johnston was back?

I jolted suddenly, realizing we hadn't told Arno about my unwelcome visitor. "We need to tell Arno that Garland Medford is here."

Hal nodded, starting the car. "I've been thinking about that. Assuming he was trying to tell us his hired killer was back, where did he get his information? Has he been tracking Johnston all this time? And, if he has, why hasn't he already taken him down for stealing his money?"

So many questions. They made my head hurt. "Maybe he's hoping Johnston will lead him to mom."

Except, if Medford really did know Johnston was the one who stole his money and botched the hit on my parents, did he really need or want to finish the job with my mom?

That last question, at least, was mildly comforting.

Hal's cell rang and he hit the Answer button. Arno's voice came through the car's speakers. "I wanted to let you know that Polly Doe jumped out of the ambulance when it reached the hospital. She's in the wind again."

"What in the world?" I muttered.

"What is going on with this woman?" Hal asked.

"Tell me what happened," Arno said.

"We found her at Angie Lucklin's house," Hal told him. "She told us quite a story."

Arno snickered. "I can't wait to hear it."

Hal repeated the interview with Polly. I inserted information here and there during his accounting of Polly's story. When we were done, Arno was silent for a moment. "If the car at Mitzner's was Lucky's, then why is his blood in the trunk? And how did the dead thug get to the garden store?"

"There must have been a second car," Hal offered.

"Then where's that car?" Arno asked.

I thought about that and had a thought. "Did your men search the auction leftovers?"

A brief silence met my question.

"Auction leftovers?" Arno finally asked.

"Yes. When my parents were..." I veered away from the word, still uncomfortable with it. "After the crash, the office manager called everyone who had items on the lot that were waiting for auction. Most people came and retrieved their items, but some didn't. The things that were left behind are all parked in the big lot at the back."

"You think the dead guy's car might be parked there?"

"It would be a good place to hide something. Nobody's gone through that stuff since...for almost three years."

"But why would Lucky hide the thug's car and leave the stolen car at Mitzner's?" Arno asked.

I didn't know the answer to that, but I could make a guess. "The Town Car was stolen, right? Lucky might have just wanted to get miles between the car and himself. Assuming that Hadley guy's car wasn't hot, it would be safer than the Lincoln."

Hal nodded. "That makes sense." He reached over and squeezed my shoulder. "Who said women weren't logical creatures?"

I smacked him on the leg and he laughed.

Arno made a harrumphing noise. "You know about the blind squirrel and the nut...right?"

"Consider yourself smacked," I told the cop.

"That would be violence against an officer of the law," he responded, a smile in his voice.

"I don't care," I told him. "It would be worth it."

"We'll meet you at the lot in fifteen minutes," Hal told Arno.

The rusted, pinkish-tan sedan didn't even stick out in the lot. Someone had parked it between a rusty old tractor and a commercial-sized snow scoop that would probably disintegrate if anyone tried to use it.

I stood back and stared at Lucky's car for a moment, shocked that my guess had been a good one.

"I guess that answers the question of why Lucky didn't want to break in," Arno said.

Hal nodded.

I looked from one man to the other, reluctant to ask them what they were talking about. Finally, it hit me. "He didn't want the police searching the lot too carefully."

Hal nodded. "It might explain the fire on the other side of the yard too. If we were focusing our attention on the annex, there'd be no reason to look at the yard full of rusty rejects over here."

"That's what I was thinking," Arno agreed. Pulling on a pair of latex gloves, he opened the car door and looked inside, giving it a thorough visual search. Finding nothing, he popped the trunk and grimaced. It was filled with what looked like dirty clothing and spoiled groceries. The stench was horrible.

Arno started pulling stuff out of the trunk,

placing it on the ground behind the car. "No bag," he said.

"Polly said there'd been a tracker in the bag," Hal reminded him. "They probably took the money out of it."

Arno tugged the carpet up and wrenched open the spare tire compartment. He whistled, reaching inside and pulling out a thick stack of bills. "Found it."

"There's one thing that doesn't make sense," I said. "If they were trying to pretend there was nothing of any interest here, then why shoot at us?" I asked.

Hal shrugged. "Maybe the shooter was afraid you'd be taking an inventory of the items in the process of putting the auction for sale. Killing us would have bought the shooter some time."

"That assumes he wanted to hide this car here for a while," Arno said. "Which also tells me he's got someone still looking for him. Or at least, for the money."

"But who?" I asked, feeling frustrated. It seemed like, whenever we figured one thing out, two more questions popped up to replace it.

Hal stood there a moment, a thoughtful look on his face, and then turned to Arno. "Do you find it interesting that Medford showed up in the middle of this?"

Arno straightened, staring down at the money

he'd uncovered. "Given that one of the victims in this was his guy, the timing couldn't be more suspect."

"Do you have enough to bring him in?" I asked.

"He'll just lawyer up," Arno said, his gaze sliding to me. "And while he's in our tender loving care in an Interview room, his thug is free to continue looking for this cash and killing anybody who gets in his way. Thereby giving him a perfect alibi."

Hal nodded his agreement. "So we should let the world know we found the money," he said, a sly glint in his intense green gaze.

Arno's brows lifted. "What exactly did you have in mind, Amity?"

"Let me make a phone call before I tell you what I'm thinking. In the meantime, why don't you bring Garland Medford in for questioning."

Arno's eyes narrowed. "Why?"

"As far as the press knows or cares, it doesn't really matter if Medford is guilty or not. Perception is all that matters. And, in this case, perception might help us hook our fish. And keep Joey and her property safe in the process."

19

Prudence Frect had bright blue eyes outlined by a dense arc of dark gold lashes. She wore her golden hair in a cute, pixy hairstyle. She was slender, perfectly proportioned, agile, and smart.

I hated her with the heat of a billion red-hot suns.

All of that lovely perfection was beyond annoying.

Or maybe it was the way she always looked at Hal as if he were a sweet, buttery Greek pastry she was willing to trash her diet for.

Having said all that, in this case I was pretty sure it was okay that Pru was there. Kind of. Since she was going to set Garland Medford back on his heels and hopefully take Hal and me out of the middle of the current mess.

I stood at the back of the crowd, just behind the

small group of news people Pru had enticed down from Indianapolis for an "impromptu" press conference about her armored car robberies.

She was standing in front of the Sheriff's Office building, her head bent intimately toward Hal's as they discussed the details of the presser. Her slim figure was perfectly adorned in a lavender-toned suit that managed to look feminine while still screaming professional. And, since the woman worked for the FBI, I knew the suit had to also be hiding a gun or two beneath its classic lines.

She probably had an eight-inch-long knife strapped to her slim, muscular thigh.

Like a dang superhero.

My lip curled and I had to force myself to uncurl it.

It didn't help that Hal was bathing her in the delicious heat of his full attention at the moment. Meanwhile, I was hiding from the press by attempting to look like a branch of the huge, potted bush behind me.

I watched as Arno strode up to them and said something that had Pru turning away from Hal and moving briskly to the spot on the wide, concrete steps where the press was waiting. She and Arno stood a couple of steps above the press as cameras whirred into focus, and lights flashed around them.

"First, I want to thank everyone for coming out today," Pru began, her manner crisp and confident.

"I know you've all been anxious about the series of armored car thefts in the state, and I wanted to disclose that there's been a break in the case."

Cameras flashed, and a low murmur broke out at the back of the group of reporters. A woman who had stick-straight blonde hair and was wearing vivid red lipstick took a step forward. "Agent Frect, has the money been recovered?"

Pru gave the woman an indulgent smile. "If you'll refrain from asking questions, I'll give you all the information I can without compromising the investigation." She waited a moment as excitement rolled through the group and flattened out, leaving them attentive and silent.

"As I was saying, we've had a break in the case. With a goal of protecting the DA's options for litigation, I'll steer clear of details that might inhibit his efforts. But I *can* tell you that we've been investigating a murder which we believe is tied to this series of crimes."

"Have you identified the victim?" a man in the back called out.

Pru smiled indulgently, a paragon of grace in the face of unprincipled scandal-seekers. "I can't give you the victim's name..."

Angry murmuring broke out.

Pru held up a hand. "But I can tell you he had significant ties to a wealthy businessman in the Indianapolis area. Our investigation is looking into that connection..."

"You're talking about Garland Medford, aren't you?" the reporter in the back yelled.

I craned my neck to see the speaker and settled my gaze on a small man with a fringe of dark hair that ran in a horseshoe shape from one oversized ear, around the bottom of his skull to the other ear. The area above the horseshoe was completely bald. From the booming sound of his voice, I'd thought he'd be much bigger.

"For obvious reasons, I can't give you the suspect's name. But I can tell you he's been summoned for questioning."

"I saw Medford's car driving through town a few minutes ago," someone called out. The statement set off an avalanche of shouted questions.

Pru waited silently, her bright gaze sliding from one reporter to the next as she folded her hands before her.

The message was clear. She wasn't going to give in to the feeding frenzy. After a few minutes, they got the message and quieted.

"Agent Frect, have you located the stolen money? We have a right to know."

Pru smiled at the man in the back. "We recovered a small amount of the cash, but we're still looking for the rest."

"How much?" a small, Asian woman called out.

"As I said, I can't give details on the case…"

"Do you have reason to believe the money's hidden here? In Deer Hollow?" the petite, dark-haired reporter asked.

Pru's expression remained unreadable. I fervently wished I could master a neutral expression like that. It would come in so handy.

"As I stated, only a portion of the money was recovered. But we're hopeful that, as we continue to investigate, we'll find the rest of the money." She threw up a hand as questions erupted again. "I'm sorry, no further questions. Thank you for coming all the way down to Deer Hollow. Have a nice day." She turned and walked with Arno back toward the Sheriff's station, disappearing inside.

A moment later, Hal strode through the mingling press and grabbed my hand. "Come on."

I started to ask him how he thought the presser had gone, but he gave his head a little shake, his gaze sliding toward the hungry reporters within hearing distance. I clamped my lips shut, intending to stay silent until we were inside the station.

It didn't quite work out that way.

"Excuse me, Miss Fulle?"

I turned to find Horseshoe Head hurrying up to me.

Alarm flashed heat into my face and made my stomach clench. I squeezed Hal's hand in desperation.

He tugged me slightly behind him, a protective maneuver I appreciated, even as I knew I couldn't let it stand. I closed my eyes for a beat and pulled air into my lungs, then stepped forward to face the man.

I was happy to see that the reporter had surrendered his microphone to his camera crew, but the aforementioned crew stood too near for my comfort, one camera still rolling.

I fixed the reporter with a hostile glare as he lumbered ungracefully to a halt before us. "Yes?"

He smiled, his wide cheeks pinching into rosy mounds on either side of a very small mouth. "Brent Maxim, Channel 5 News. How are you today?"

"What can we help you with, Mr. Maxim?" Hal asked. His tone was cool but not hostile, though I knew that could change at the drop of a hat. Reporters weren't Hal's favorite thing.

Mine either. They'd pursued me relentlessly after the plane crash, seemingly unconcerned about my broken heart and terror for the future.

Maxim kept his gaze locked on me. "I wanted to get your reaction to Garland Medford's connection in this case. That must be shocking, given his involvement in your parents' deaths?"

Cognizant of the rolling camera not too far away, and the leading aspect to the reporter's question, I tried to keep my expression neutral. The man had put me in a terrible position. Pru had carefully worded her statement to the press to avoid naming

Medford specifically while giving enough information to the slavering press to let them know she was referring to him. She was walking a legal tightrope. One I had no intention of knocking her off of. I cocked my head, giving Maxim a confused look. "I didn't hear Mr. Medford's name mentioned. If I had, I would certainly be alarmed." I smiled. "As you can imagine."

Maxim nodded eagerly. "It's true that Agent Frect didn't mention Medford by name, but it was clear to everyone who she was talking about. Is that why you're here? Are you going to observe the interrogation?"

I didn't miss how he'd exchanged the word *interview* for the more dire sounding *interrogation*.

"As I said, I have no idea who Agent Frect's suspect is. I look forward to hearing all about it when you report it." I smiled. "Now, if you'll excuse me?"

"Don't you find it a little surprising that Medford arrived in Deer Hollow in the midst of all this? That he showed up at your home?"

The toe of my shoe caught in a crack of the sidewalk and I stumbled. Hal caught me under the arm as anger washed through me. I spun, barely stopping myself from snarling. "Are you watching my house, Mr. Maxim?"

Beside me, Hal stiffened, and I realized my mistake.

The smug smile on the reporter's small mouth confirmed it. "So you admit he was there? Did he threaten you too? Are you afraid he'll kill you the way he killed your parents?"

Maxim had been making an educated guess. Probably based on the fact that he and the rest of the press had studied Medford exhaustively. No doubt they'd been digging into his businesses, background, and proclivities with the zeal of those hoping to find something...anything...they could use to smear the highly successful businessman.

I checked that thought, realizing with a start that I was dangerously close to sympathizing with Medford. Maybe because I was currently getting a small taste of that seek and destroy mentality.

The front door of the Sherriff's headquarters opened and Deputy Schmidt came outside. Her attractive face wore a cop's neutral expression, and her gaze was tight with displeasure as it slid to Maxim. "Ms. Fulle, Mr. Amity, Deputy Willager would like to speak with you."

Without another word, I turned on my heel and headed for the deputy. Hal hung back a couple of steps, no doubt intending to form a barrier between the nosy reporter and me. It was a nice thought. But the damage had already been done.

I shook like I'd been caught naked in an ice storm. The reporter's careless questions had stripped me bare, shoving me nearly off my foundation. He'd ripped a chunk of my hard-won confidence away and unsettled my newly-framed world with a brutality that matched my father's loss.

Tears burned my gaze as fear scraped along my nerve endings with every shouted question Maxim continued to propel my way.

Without any real effort on his part, the unpleasant man had dragged me backward in time. Into the icy ruthlessness of the days following my father's violent death and the subsequent loss of everything I'd ever known and loved.

I only hoped our gambit had been worth it. Because it already felt as if Garland Medford had won.

20

"What do we do now?" I asked. I huddled in a chair in the corner of Arno's office, holding a Styrofoam cup of bad coffee between my hands as if I needed it to keep them from freezing.

Arno stood at the window, hands in pockets and his back to us. He seemed engrossed in watching the cars flash past on the busy highway.

Pru was on her cell phone in the hallway, presumably filling her boss in on our attempted sting operation.

Hal leaned against the wall nearby, his intense green gaze swinging worriedly to me as I continued to struggle against my demons.

Arno glanced at his watch. "We wait. Pru's got people on the trailer and the auction." His head snapped around. "I can put somebody at your house too if you want."

I lifted my gaze and shook my head. "No. But thanks."

"She's coming to my house," Hal said.

I opened my mouth to argue, but he shook his head. "It's either that, or I'm sleeping on your couch again. I'm not leaving you alone."

"This isn't about me," I objected weakly. But I didn't fight him hard. I understood his need to keep an eye on me. I didn't really mind. It just rankled that nobody ever thought I could take care of myself.

The door opened and Pru came inside. "Medford's already called my boss." She winced. "Apparently, they're racquetball besties."

"Wonderful," I murmured.

She sent me a murderous look that I was pretty sure wasn't directed at me. "I'm to pull back immediately. Disband the operation."

Arno didn't look surprised, which explained why he'd been staring into space for the last several minutes. He nodded. "It's no more than we expected," he said, surprising me.

"Wait," I said, sitting straighter in my chair. "You knew this would fail?"

"Fail? No," Pru responded. "But we made a conscious decision to ask for forgiveness rather than permission."

I glanced at Hal and he shrugged. "You knew?"

"Not the details," he said. "But I understand the

political quagmire here. It's how Medford has skated for this long."

"I'm slightly out of my jurisdiction here," Pru stated. "Medford has been suspected of crimes across state lines, so I've been able to carve a narrow niche out for myself in monitoring his operations. But, I've gotten a lot of push-back from the higher-ups."

"Fortunately, the perception of illegality has been created," Arno told me. "Medford can try to stop us, but he can't do anything about public opinion."

I gave up on the bad coffee, setting the cup on the floor next to my chair. "So, I guess I'll repeat my question. What do we do now?"

"Now, you go home," Arno said. "And Pru will monitor the auction lot."

I frowned at the FBI agent. "But I thought you said you had to stop?"

Her smile was tight. "It's probably going to take me a while to find my guys and read them in once I get there. If the thief should show up while I'm there..." She shrugged.

Arno nodded. "I'm seeing a flat tire and engine trouble in your future."

I snorted.

Hal touched my arm. "Come on, honey. I know a pig who probably thinks the world has ended about now. It's been almost two hours since she last ate."

Pru's smile turned genuine at the mention of Ethel Squeaks, and it made me like her better. "The pot-bellied pig you rescued at Christmas time?" She laughed. "I guess I never saw you as a pig guy."

Hal's chuckle was filled with affection. "I'd be proud to be a pig guy. In fact, I started out as one. But I've kind of lost custody of my little pot belly."

I patted his stomach. "Hang with me long enough and it will definitely come back."

Even Arno laughed at that.

Hal shook Pru's hand. "Let me know if you need help."

"I will."

He nodded to Arno. "Deputy. Debrief later?"

"I'll let you know how everything turns out."

I was silent on the way home, my thoughts scattered and my emotions confused. It felt strange to be going home to feed my pets and have a quiet evening when Arno and Pru would be fighting a battle that felt like mine.

I kept reminding myself it wasn't really my battle. Because it wasn't. It had started on my property, but I had no reason to think it had anything to do with me.

No reason at all.

So why did I feel as if it did?

"Penny for your thoughts?" Hal said, squeezing my icy hand in his big, warm one.

I sighed. "Nothing. I think I'm just tired."

"Tired and worried about everything?"

I nodded. "Maybe a little."

"You think we should be involved." It wasn't a question.

My head snapped around and he nodded. "I'm feeling the same way."

"Then let's go out there. To the auction. They might need our..." I flushed, realizing how stupid it was to assume they'd need my help for anything. "...your help."

He shook his head. "I'm where I want to be. Pru and Arno are trained for this kind of thing. They'll be fine."

He was right. I knew he was. But I couldn't help feeling as if we were missing something important.

Hal turned the SUV into my driveway, the headlights sweeping across the pond as he turned. The glow temporarily illuminated a deer and her baby drinking on the far side.

"Aw, look at tha...ah!"

A woman dove in front of the car, her face a ghostly white in the headlights.

Hal slammed his foot down on the brakes and the car skidded violently on the gravel drive. The back end slid sideways before he managed to stop its forward momentum, mere inches from a pasty-faced Polly.

She slapped her hands on the hood of the car as Hal jammed it into Park and we climbed out.

"Are you okay?" I asked, concerned by the terror in her face and the tears in her eyes. "Thank goodness I found you," Polly said, grasping my hands as I hurried around the car. "I'm so scared. I don't know what to do."

"It's going to be okay," I told her, giving her icy hands a squeeze. "Just tell us what's wrong."

"He..." She scraped a hand over her face, leaving behind a smear of fresh blood. I gave her a closer look in the headlights. She'd found a flannel shirt somewhere, a man's shirt from the look of it, and the front was dark with blood. I wondered how much of the stuff she could lose before she passed out. It seemed like every time I saw her, more blood was leaking out. "He threatened my brother. I have to do what he wants. I don't know how to save him."

"Your brother?" Hal asked, grabbing her arm as she wavered on her feet.

Polly turned a tear-filled gaze to him, nodding.

"Who's threatening your brother, Polly?" I asked.

Polly shook her head. "I can't tell you. He'll kill me."

Panic making her sob, she gripped my hands so tightly the bones creaked. "Okay, that's fine. How can we help?"

Polly sniffed loudly, finally letting go of me to wipe her nose on the sleeve of the long-suffering flannel. "I need to give him the money or he's gonna kill George..."

I blinked in surprise. "George?" Realization struck. "George Burrows?"

She nodded, wringing her hands together. "Lucky went to him when he realized he was in trouble. George wouldn't help him. He said that Lucky had gotten himself into trouble and he could get himself out." Her expression clearly showed her rage. "Unfortunately for George, they saw Lucky leaving his house. They thought Lucky had given George the money." She shook her head. "George is a jerk, but he's my brother."

"So you're Polly Burrows?" I asked. So much for the Burrows daughter being the only one to make something of herself. "The doctor from Indianapolis?"

She frowned. "Nurse, actually. Unemployed. And I go by the name of Hadley. My mother's maiden name."

Hadley? Where had I heard that before?

"Where are they keeping George?" Hal asked the distraught woman.

"They grabbed him at his house, but I don't know where they took him. They made him call me because they knew I wouldn't come otherwise. They said to get the money and bring it to the plant store where we dumped the car."

"Mizner's?"

She nodded, sniffling loudly. "That's the place they said."

Hal looked at me, his expression filled with concern. I was pretty sure I knew what he was thinking. Pru and Arno were looking for Medford in the wrong spot.

"Do you think it's Johnston?" I asked.

Hal frowned. "I guess it's possible. But something feels off."

"Are you going to help me, or not," Polly asked, becoming more agitated.

I eyed her, wondering at her emotional state. I couldn't help speculating about what she wasn't telling us. "What did you have in mind?"

Did Polly think Hal and I had the money?

"I know where the money is. I need you to call off the cops so I can get it."

"How long have you known?" I asked her.

Her gaze shifted away.

"If you want our help, you need to be honest with us, Polly," Hal said.

Her fingers twined rapidly together, her chest heaving. "Lucky told me where he hid it. He thought it would be safe there for a long time. But when I saw that you were sellin' the place, I panicked. I told him we needed to move it." She swallowed hard.

"Somehow, they found him before he could get the money out of there and they killed him." Tears glistened in her eyes. "I can't help thinking that if I'd have just left it alone, he'd have been fine."

"But I thought he was staying there," I said.

"He had been. After the killer caught him trying to bury the money at that plant place, he decided he needed a better spot to hide it. He didn't know if the guy had reported back to his boss in Indy. So he hid it at the auction and stayed there to protect it. But that day...the day he was..." She swallowed hard again. "He'd come to the trailer to see me. Somebody must have followed him back."

I suddenly remembered where I'd heard the name Hadley before. Realization twisted painfully in my chest. Polly was lying to us.

Hal realized it too. His hand slid to the gun he kept in the small of his back. "The thug at the plant store was identified, Polly. Do you know his name?"

She slid a confused look his way. She was a good actress. "Name? No, why should I?"

"His name was Bob Hadley."

I watched her carefully, seeing the confusion morph into surprise and then pain. She had to have known, but she was a darn fine actress. Maybe she'd have been better off to go into acting instead of nursing.

She seemed to crumple and Hal instinctively reached for her. Polly straightened suddenly, her head connecting with Hal's chin and knocking him backward. As he slammed against the hood, she kicked his gun away from him and yanked her own weapon from beneath the bloody flannel. "Pim's dead?"

She sounded so broken, I almost believed her. "Polly, the police are in place at Fulle Proof. You won't get away with the money."

"I have to. George..."

Hal straightened, looking a little wobbly from the blow to his jaw. "Stop the lies, Polly," he ground out. The stark illumination of the headlights showed a line of blood trickling down his chin. "George isn't in trouble. This is over. Give me the gun."

She shook her head, eyes bright with some emotion. Reaching into the pocket of her jeans, she pulled out her cell. "He is! They sent me this." She woke the cell and pressed an app with her thumb, bringing up a picture. She held it up to show us.

It could have been George. He'd been beaten so badly it was hard to know for sure. He was sitting in a chair, his face bloated and purple. One eye was swollen nearly shut and blood trailed from his temple.

Well, that certainly clouded the issue.

"Did you speak to somebody, or did they just send you a text?" Hal asked her.

"They just sent this picture. I tried calling George

and there was no answer. So I grabbed a gun and headed out..."

Hal held up a hand. "Where'd you get a gun? The last time we met, you were passed out in an ambulance. How did you get here?"

She shrugged. "Not important. The short version is that I was tired of your questions."

My mouth fell open. She hadn't passed out. She'd been faking so we'd call an ambulance and she could escape. The dirty dog!

"Did you know I used to be an EMT? I know my way around ambulances. I helped myself to some pain meds and antibiotics before I got out of there."

"You are hard to keep in one place," Hal said, shaking his head.

"If it was your family being threatened, you wouldn't have done the same?" she asked, her tone bitter.

Hal sighed. "Okay, we're back to square one." He eyed her weapon. "Why don't you give me that gun?"

Polly shook her head. "Not happenin'. If you aren't going to help me, I might need it."

"We'll help you save your brother," Hal said. "But we're going to have to do it without the money. I'm not going to help you steal that cash."

Polly sneered. "But you'll let your cop friends help themselves, won't you?"

"What are you talking about?" I asked.

Polly's glance was filled with hate. "Lucky and I

stole that money. You don't think I know how much was there. I saw that FBI witch on TV. She said they'd recovered some of it but were still looking for the rest. I know how that's going to go down. The money will mysteriously not be found. Somebody's going to have sticky fingers."

I pressed my lips together on a desire to tell her it had been part of the plan to draw the killer out. I didn't want Arno and yes, even Pru, to be painted as dirty cops. But there'd been a reason they'd decided to spread the false information. I wasn't going to be the one to disrupt the plan.

Hal shook his head. "Maybe Lucky spent some of it."

Polly snorted. "While hiding out in an empty building? I don't think so."

"Maybe he split it up and hid some of it in a different spot," I said, my gaze skimming to Hal's. "Do you know of any other spot where he might have hidden some of the money?"

Polly shook her head. "No. Lucky wouldn't have split the money up."

She was either very sure of Lucky, or just too stubborn to consider another option. Either way, we weren't going to get any further with her on that subject.

Hal held out his hand. "Give me your phone. I'll have the police trace the sender and then we'll know who has George."

"What good will that do me?" Polly sneered. "He'll still be in danger. I already lost one brother. I'm not losing another one."

"It will help us figure out where he might be," Hal said, using his most persuasive tone.

But Polly wasn't having any of it. She compressed her lips into a mulish look. Waving the gun toward the car, she said. "Leave your phones on the ground and climb into the car. You're driving, Amity. If you don't try anything stupid, I won't shoot your girl-friend in the head."

21

Hal stopped the car on a dark gravel road behind the auction lot. When he glanced my way, Polly sat forward and pressed the muzzle of the gun against my head. "Eyes forward and keep your hands on the wheel," she barked.

He looked into the rear-view mirror at her. "This place is crawling with Feds. If we go sneaking in the back, we're going to get shot. Even if you live through it, you won't get your money."

Polly gave him a grim smile. "*We* won't get shot. *You* will. Unless you use all that sneakiness you've learned through being a cop and then a private investigator. Your little girlfriend and I will be waiting here. If you don't come back with the money, she's dead."

I reached for him, panic swirling in my gut. "No! He'll be killed."

Polly fixed me with an icy glare. "If he's shot, it'll be a nice distraction for me, won't it?"

I realized she was hoping Hal would get shot so she could sneak in and get the money. Evil.

He leaned close and kissed me before Polly could react.

She slammed the gun against the top of the seat, startling us out of the kiss. "No touching. Now get in there. I'll be watching you, Amity. If you try to call out to the cops, she'll be dead before they even get out here."

Hal grasped my hand as he pulled back and left something hard and warm in it as he pulled away. His gaze was filled with love. "Stay safe," he told me.

Tears slid down my cheeks as I realized it might be the last time I saw him. I reached out as he slipped from the car, but Polly's hand snaked through the seats and grabbed my wrist. In a panic, I released the small knife he'd slipped into my hand, thinking she was going to find it. It slipped between the seat and the console with a small thud.

Thrashing against her hold, I kicked the underneath of the dashboard to cover the small sound.

Polly wrenched my inside arm around, twisting me brutally in the seat, and zip-stripped me to the "holy hotrod" handle in the ceiling. "Don't make a sound or your boyfriend's not going to make it out of there," she threatened. Then she hesitated, looking at me, her eyes glossy with some kind of emotion in the dim light. "Look, I just want what's mine. I'm sorry to drag you into this. I really tried not to. But I didn't see any way around it."

Her apology meant nothing to me. She'd just sent the man I loved into a death trap. "If something happens to him, I'm going to make sure you pay."

She shrugged. "Join the club. I'm getting pretty used to people bangin' on me." She pulled something from the waistband of her jeans and tugged it over her bright hair, tucking he long strands out of sight. Then she climbed out of the Escalade and disappeared into the darkness.

I listened for a long moment, comforted by the silence. No gunfire meant that nobody was shooting at Hal.

I tried to retrieve the knife but couldn't reach it with my arm twisted across my body and lifted above my head. I'd need to untwist first. I unclasped my seat belt and maneuvered around until I faced the back seat.

Panting from my efforts, I stretched my free hand toward the space between the seat and the console, praying the knife hadn't fallen all the way to the floor.

My fingers slipped inside and I shifted them from side to side.

Nothing.

I strained toward the narrow space, groaning in pain as my shoulder threatened to pop from its socket. I had a thought that I might be able to break the zip strip if I pulled hard enough, but no such luck. The thick, plastic strip held.

Finally, my shoulder screaming under the strain, my fingers touched the warm metal. I tried to grip it with my fingertips. It slipped sideways, evading my grasp. Sweat broke out on my forehead, dripping down to my chin, as I stretched. After several long moments, I managed to get my fingertips on the knife.

But I couldn't grasp it. It kept slipping from my grip. So I went with Plan B. I found the warm metal again and tried pushing it toward the front of the seat.

It slid, slipped, and sunk slightly deeper toward the floor. I gave a frustrated cry, pounding on the back of the seat.

Gritting my teeth, I tried again, unwilling to give up on Hal. Much straining and grunting later, I got my fingertips on the knife again.

Gunfire burst into the quiet night.

I jumped, gave a little scream, and in full-on panic, gritted my teeth and shoved, hitting the end of the knife and pushing it hard. It clattered to the floor of the car and I dove for it.

A moment later, I'd cut myself free and scrambled out of the SUV with the knife still clutched in my hand.

I started running in the direction Polly had gone

as gunfire flared through the night, the sound of bullets pinging off metal a near-constant refrain.

"Hal, Hal, Hal, Hal..." I chanted as I ran, tears sliding down my cheeks. I was going to be too late. I knew it. And he would be killed.

Rage mingled with fear to increase my speed. Ahead of me, I saw the gap in the fencing that Hal had made by ripping the chain link away from the supporting post and bending it to make room for him to shimmy underneath.

A pain-filled cry speared through the night. I jolted to a stop. "Hal!"

Fear made my heart pound against my chest. Pinpricks of silvery light danced across my vision. I tensed, fully intending to follow Hal into the now-silent auction lot to find him.

But things didn't quite go as planned.

As I started forward, the night swung sideways and a tall form rose up beside me. Before I even had time to call out, something bit my throat. Everything started to whirl.

The ground spun up to find me, smacking me hard in the face, and the strong scent of rich earth filled my pain-filled senses. I rolled to my back, seeing the shadowed form of my attacker standing over me as the night blurred, and then fell away.

My first awareness was a distant droning sound. My second was the cold draft of air passing over me, smelling of rotting vegetation and fish.

My head pounded and my neck was stiff. When I tried to lift my head, pain screeched through my neck and pulsed through my shoulders.

I tried to lift a hand to rub the ache and pain sliced through my wrists.

My arm wouldn't move. I was tied down. Trapped!

I opened my eyes and tried to take in my surroundings.

In the distance, a horn honked. Then there was only the far away murmur of rushing water. Scanning the darkened room, I saw the jagged edges of glass outlining the room's only window. Broken. That seemed important somehow, but my mind was too muzzy to grasp how.

Icy air spun through the room from the ruptured glass, turning my skin numb with cold.

I shivered violently, realizing I'd been trembling for a while. My hands and feet were numb from the cold.

My eyes caught on a dark spot on the floor. Memory flashed. I suddenly knew where I was.

But why?

There could only be one explanation. "Polly!" I called out, listening for footsteps.

"Polly! Dangit! Let me go."

Silence met my demand. I realized she hadn't put anything over my mouth. Which meant she wasn't worried about anybody hearing me. That added weight to my theory of where I was. "Polly!"

Footsteps finally sounded on the other side of the door. It opened slowly, revealing a tall figure who was backlit by the soft glow of a camping lantern.

My captor hadn't wanted to use too many lights. Would lights be noticed? Maybe we weren't too far from other homes after all.

I narrowed my gaze on the figure in the door. Something was off about it. Something had changed. I lifted my chin. "Let me go. We did everything you asked us to do."

The figure stood there a moment, features hidden by the dark permeating most of the home. After a few tense beats, my captor stepped into the room with me, giving me a view of the next room.

I gasped, my pulse spiking. And everything fell into place. I knew who'd killed Pim Burrows. I knew who'd killed Polly. And I knew who was probably going to kill me.

"What did you do to her?" I asked Angie Lucklin.

Polly sat on the floor beneath a large window directly across from me. Her head rested on her chest and her thick torso was drenched in blood.

She wasn't moving. Her chest didn't show any evidence of rising and falling. "You killed her?"

The figure leaned against the wall next to the door, arms crossed.

Though I couldn't see it through the dark, I couldn't help feeling as if Angie was smiling, amused by my questions.

Finally, she spoke, confirming my guess about her identity. "She killed herself. But I'm glad she's dead," Angie said. I watched her shoulders shrug, the action of a cold, uncaring killer.

I shook my head. "Why?"

"Such an interesting question. One with so many possible responses. First, she deserved it for killing my boy."

"Polly killed Lucky?"

Another shrug. "As good as. They turned against him. Her and that horrible brother of hers. They wanted all the money for themselves. But Lance was too smart for them. He wouldn't tell them where the money was because he didn't trust them."

Angie straightened against the wall and moved closer, her face finally illuminated by the ray of light from the other room. "Polly didn't know my Lance as well as she thought she did, or she'd have figured it out. I did. As soon as I learned there'd been money, I knew. He wouldn't have let it out of his sight. If he was staying at that auction, he'd hidden it there. Then I saw his car and I knew."

"How'd you find out?" I asked. "About the money?"

She jerked a gaze to the other room. For a moment, I thought she'd heard something, but she shook her head. "That stupid girl told me. She was screaming about not knowing where it was when I was trying to kill her." Angie laughed. "When she got away and managed to survive like the cockroach she was, I decided to keep her around for a while, hoping she'd find the money. Turned out I didn't need her. I figured out where it was myself."

"That's why you were there that day? The day you set fire to the annex and shot at us?" I was guessing, but remembering what she'd told us about going to the academy...about being good at only one thing...made it a likely scenario.

Her expression told me I'd gotten it right. "When I saw you there, I panicked a little. I was afraid you'd find the car and discover the money." She shook her head. "I couldn't let you do that. My boy died for that money. It was his."

I bit back the urge to accuse her of wanting it for herself. It wouldn't buy me anything to enrage her. "So, you tried to kill us."

She shrugged again. "I really didn't have any idea of killing you. I just wanted to keep you focused on that building. Once everyone cleared out, I intended to go back and get the money."

"Why didn't you come back for it?"

She blew out a frustrated breath. "I should have. But, when you and that handsome PI of yours came to me, asking questions about the Burrows and Indianapolis, I thought you'd be off investigating the wrong people in the wrong places for a while. I figured I had some time. The money was safe there from the girl. And her rotten brother wasn't going to get it. He was already dead." She sniffed. "The boy could change his name, but he shouldn't have forgotten his roots. He should have remembered about small towns. Nothing stays hidden in places like Deer Hollow unless you take great care to make sure they do."

I frowned. "What do you mean?"

"A few days ago, a friend of mine mentioned she saw Pim Burrows drive up to the old auction and wondered if Lance was in town too. That made me curious. I'd been trying to call Lance for a couple of days because he'd told me he was coming home for a while. But then I didn't hear from him again. Knowing he and Pim were tight, I thought maybe the two of them were up to something. So I went to the auction and broke through the fence in the back." She shuddered, wrapping her arms around herself. "I found him in that building and I knew who'd killed him." She slid a murderous glance toward Polly. "I went lookin' for that little thug. Saw him comin' out of the liquor store. You know the one off Jamison street? They have some great deals on hard liquor."

I stared at her until she looked away. For a minute she seemed to have forgotten we weren't best buddies having tea together.

"Anyway, I followed him back to the plant place and killed him. But not until after I got him to tell me everything."

"You got Pim Burrows to tell you everything that happened?" I let disbelief color my tone, hoping it would make her determined to tell me the rest of the story.

"The little thug was very talkative once I had him hogtied in that forklift."

"He admitted they were trying to cut Lance out of the money?"

Angie nodded. "Burrows had known about that theft ring for a while. He and Lance cooked up the idea of taking the money from the thieves. Burrows said it was a small group of independents, with no organization or muscle behind them. He thought they'd write it off as a loss and move on. He didn't believe they'd come after the money. But, just in case, they put Lance at the front of it. They let him be the only one the cops saw that day. They set him up for the fall. Unfortunately, Lance was too much in love with the girl to recognize what they were doing. But when push came to shove, my boy knew enough not to trust those two. Once they got here, he hid the money and wouldn't tell them where it was."

"Didn't they know it was in the car?" George Burrows said Lucky had the Chevy when he saw him at the auction. Polly had to know the car was on the lot.

She shook her head. "Lance told them he'd dumped the car in the reservoir and buried the money at the plant place. Pim attacked him, tried to make him dig it up. But Lance got away somehow and he was safe for a while. Until he trusted that stupid girl with his location. Then they killed him."

"What was Pim doing at Mitzner's that day, when you...found him?" I asked.

"Fool was still looking for the money. He was convinced Lucky'd hid it there."

"And Lucky's blood on the Town Car?"

She shrugged. "Burrows said they fought and Pim managed to hit him with the shovel and get away. Maybe the blood got on the car during that fight."

If Lucky was bleeding and picked up the shovel to hit Pim, that would explain how his blood got on the shovel handle.

My head ached from thinking about the ugly mess, but I had to keep Angie talking. Maybe if I stalled long enough, someone would figure out where we were.

"Did you kill George Burrows too?" I was half

afraid to know the answer to that. But, in for a penny...

She scrunched up her face. "George? Why would I kill him?"

"Polly showed us what somebody did to him. He looked bad."

Angie laughed gaily. "Oh, that. I told her to use that picture to get you to help. He sent me that when he was trying to sue me to pay for motorcycle repairs."

I had to think about that for a beat and then remembered. "When he crashed into your car."

She nodded. "I don't know why I kept that picture. It enraged me at the time that the little jerk was trying to shake me down. But it did come in handy."

"Then, George isn't involved at all?"

"Not as far as I know."

I tugged uselessly on the strips binding me to the arms and legs of the chair, trying to keep the movements small so she wouldn't notice in the dark.

Unfortunately, I wasn't having much luck. They barely loosened from my efforts.

"Polly said she came to you for help," I said, trying to keep her talking.

"She did. When she showed up on my doorstep, I figured she knew I'd been the one to attack her. But she told me she was in trouble. That Lance had told her to come to me if she needed help. But I knew as soon as I spoke to her that she was much more worried about the money than my boy. I realized then that I could use her to get Lance's money. I'd honor him by not letting his killers get his rightful inheritance."

"If that's what helps you sleep at night," I murmured.

She cocked her head. "You think I wanted that cash for myself." It wasn't a question, so I didn't treat it as one. "Don't you?"

She turned to look through the broken glass, seeming to fall into her thoughts. A moment later, she said, "When Lance's dad died, I thought my life would be better. It wasn't that he was a bad man. He was just always judging me, making demands. There wasn't a day that went by when I didn't wish I could just be alone in that old farmhouse. Just spend my days like I wanted to spend them. Grabbing every moment for myself." She sighed. "But old farmhouses fall apart. Things need to be updated. I realized how nice it would be to have a little more money." Her gaze slid back to me. "I think that's why he did it," she said. "I think he took that money for me."

"The people he stole that money from will come after it, once they know where it is. Even if you ended up with it, you'd have to go on the run." I didn't know if that was true or not, but I didn't want her to get too comfortable with the idea of keeping it.

"You do speak from experience on that, don't you, dear?" Angie said in a saccharine sweet voice. "Your parents crossed the wrong man in Garland Medford, and they paid the price for it, didn't they?"

I glared at her, not bothering to correct her assumptions. "You'd do well to learn from their mistakes." Even after almost three years, I still had no idea if she was right about that.

Angie seemed amused. "I'm not your parents, Joey. I know the system. I've been inside. And I know for a fact that nobody's going to come after me for that money."

"How could you possibly know that?"

She actually laughed. "Lovely Agent Prucilla Frect made sure of that for me. Garland Medford would be crazy to insert himself into this now. The Feds are all over him and his business. He's not going to risk prison for a measly couple of million dollars." She shook her head. "No, I'm heading to a beach some-where far away. I'll get myself a cute little villa on the beach and sip girly drinks for the rest of my life."

The woman was cray-cray. "You need to get the money first."

She laughed, turning to point to a large duffel bag sitting on the floor beneath the lantern. "I already have it. Thanks to your delicious Mr. Amity."

She made a pouty face. "It's really too bad about him. He was such a handsome man."

Pure, jagged terror speared through me. It was an actual physical pain twisting my belly into a massive knot. All the blood ran from my face and the room started to spin. "What do you mean?"

Angie walked over to the shadowed spot near the door and reached for something. She came up with a long gun, probably a hunting rifle if I had to guess. Like nearly everyone else in Deer Hollow, I was guessing the Lucklins enjoyed hunting in the woods on their acreage.

"Tell me!" I screamed, suddenly at the end of my patience. "What happened to Hal?"

Angie checked the chamber on the rifle, taking her time just to terrorize me. Finally, she looked up. "Dead, dear. I'm really sorry." Only she wasn't. She actually looked amused. "But he was very useful. He did his job well. He was a stellar distraction."

Despair washed over me, yanking all the strength from my limbs. The world spun and I had to close my eyes for fear I'd pass out again.

Nausea bloomed fast and bright through my belly. I retched violently, but nothing came up. "You killed him..." I shoved ruthlessly at the devastation waiting to take me down to my knees. The only way I could keep it at bay was to embrace the rage fighting for dominance. I threw myself forward. "You killed him!"

Angie winced as the chair legs slammed back to the floor. "Actually, the police killed him." She smiled again. "I really am sorry about that. But the good news is that you won't have to live without him for very long." Her smile brightened as she lifted the gun, sighting me with it. "Not long at all. In fact, you'd already be dead if it wasn't for that one..." She slid another glare in Polly's direction. "She seemed to think you'd be useful as a hostage. Stupid girl." Then she smiled, a wide, guileless curve of lips that pretty much proved she was mad as a hatter. "It has been handy having a nurse around, though. Such lovely drugs. I made sure to keep some for myself. Like I kept my husband's old drugs. They come in handy when you least expect it, you know."

Out of the corner of my eye, I saw a dark form appear in the door behind Angie. It was a tall form, strong and masculine. Hope flared as the form leaped toward Angie, one hand yanking the rifle up as she fired and the other punching her hard in the temple. She sagged downward, folding to the floor like a heavy drapery.

I squinted into the shadows, my heart pounding hard. "Hal?" Even as I said his name, I knew there was no hope it was him. He was dead.

My chest tightened to the point I couldn't draw a breath.

Angie lay motionless as the form bent over her. I

heard the soft sound of a zip strip before he straightened.

He moved quickly toward me, finally emerging into the light.

I gasped, shrinking back in the chair.

Garland Medford followed my horrified gaze to the rifle in his gloved hands. He frowned as if he'd just realized he was holding it. "Oh. Sorry." He set it on the ground and kicked it away. Then he bent over me, wincing as I tried frantically to put distance between us. "I'm not here to hurt you, Joey," he said, sounding offended.

He pulled a knife from his pocket and flipped it open. Ignoring my yelp of fear, he sliced efficiently through the strips. Then he handed me a cell phone. "It's a burner. Call Amity. Tell him where you are."

He straightened and headed toward the front room. Medford stopped in the doorway and looked back. "I don't want to hurt your mother, Joey. I know she's alive, and I know she had nothing to do with Sasha's death." Sasha was the woman who'd supposedly stolen money from him. My parents had been protecting her from Medford when my father and Sasha had been killed in a suspicious plane crash.

I'd always thought Garland had been behind that crash.

I blinked at him. "Why should I believe that?"

"I don't blame you if you don't. I know it looks bad. But there are things you don't know. Dangerous things. I just wanted to tell you that you have nothing to fear from me."

I shook my head, not ready to let go of years of suspicion and fear.

Garland stared at me for a long moment and then turned away. He strode quickly to the bag of money on the floor and grabbed it. But, he hesitated a moment more before leaving. "I'm glad your mom wasn't on that plane, Joey. Whether you believe me or not." And then he was gone.

I stood there, completely dazed for a moment as he left, and then shook it off and ran after him. I ran out the front door of the tiny home and into the night, looking around for Garland. He was nowhere in sight.

No headlights illuminated the long drive.

There were no tires crunching over the gravel.

I didn't hear him moving through the dense woods surrounding the home. No dried leaves crackling under heavy boots. No sticks crunching underfoot.

It was as if he'd just disappeared.

Then I heard the faint whomp, whomp, whomp of helicopter blades, and turned toward the distant sound. Pinpoint yellow lights flashed through the night and a much brighter light flared into view. I stood watching as the chopper rolled into a wide turn and disappeared into the black night.

I looked down at the phone in my hand and,

Medford's instructions finally sank in. Excitement flared through me. I quickly dialed Hal's number.

It rang several times before I got his voice mail.

Hope crashed around my feet. Tears burned in my eyes and my legs gave out beneath me. I hit the grass hard, air slamming out of my chest as I began to sob.

Hal was gone.

Medford had either lied cruelly to me, or he hadn't known.

I rolled into the fetal position, crying until I couldn't cry any longer. I had to get the police out to the house. Angie Lucklin was inside. And Polly.

Shoving myself off the ground, I scrubbed tears out of my eyes so I could read the numbers on the phone, and started stabbing out Arno's number.

The burner phone rang, a familiar number like a beacon across its face.

Sucking in a breath, I hit the *Answer* button. "Hal?"

"Joey, thank goodness. Where are you?"

22

I stood staring at the burnt husk of the annex, my feelings a jumbled mix that had me in turns wanting to roll into the fetal position and bawl, and fighting the urge to just bargain-basement the whole place and be done with it.

Somewhere deep in my core I knew I'd never truly be able to get on with my life until the auction moved on. In whatever form it was destined to take.

Hal was talking on his phone as he approached, his midnight hair glossy and painted in blue highlights in the bright sun. Caphy bounced along beside him, tongue lolling and bright green gaze perpetually sliding to check on her best friend. Ethel's ears twitched happily, her little snout snorfling along the rocks looking for scraps of food, and her little tail spinning like a top.

It had been Hal's idea to bring the pig along with

us. With the gate closed, she was perfectly safe in the lot, and it was good for her to get some exercise and fresh air.

Plus, she'd been clingy like plastic wrap since the night I'd been drugged and kidnapped and found myself alone with a dead woman and a crazy lady.

The little pig seemed to sense how much the night had affected me. Especially my terror that I'd lost Hal. I still suffered some residual effects of that night. If I went too long without seeing him, panic tried to reassert itself and I found myself seeking him out for reassurance.

I admired him for a moment before closing my eyes and letting the happily singing birds and warmth of the day fill me with peace.

"Thanks, Ben. I look forward to it." Hal disconnected and gave me a smile. "The construction crew will be here in the morning. Ben thinks it'll take about a week to do the repairs. His bid for the job is better than the other three, so I told him we looked forward to working with him. I hope you don't mind my making the decision."

I shook my head. "No. I'm glad. Thanks for helping me with that."

"My pleasure. I actually worked with Ben on the cabin and was hoping he would work out. He does good work."

Hal had bought the property next to mine after our first investigation together. At the time, it had been a dilapidated cabin in the woods, with a broken-down still in the yard. With the talented Ben and a lot of good taste, my PI had turned it into a comfy getaway.

He'd also planted daisies in the still.

I slid my arms around his waist and laid my head on his chest with a sigh. Hal kissed the top of my head and held me, letting silence embrace us for a long moment as if he knew I needed it.

Then, putting the last of the melancholy behind me, I stepped away. "Shall we go get the rest of the packing done?"

We started toward the office building, Caphy bouncing along beside us. Ethel lagged behind, her snout buried in a thick patch of weeds. "Come on, Ethel Squeaks!" I called out. I turned and walked backward, watching her ignore me. "You're going to miss out on the snack I brought for you."

Her head snapped up and she gave a little squeal, her tiny hooves spewing rock dust as she ran.

I didn't speak pig, and she didn't really understand English. But, apparently, the word "snack" was universal across species.

Caphy and LaLee certainly understood it.

A horn sounded at the front gate. We turned to see Arno in his Sheriff's car, waiting for us to open up for him.

"It's unlocked!" Hal called out.

As I got the animals safely inside, Hal waited for

Arno to open the gate and drive through. A moment later, the two men came into the building together.

Unable to ignore my pushy pets, Arno bent to pet Caphy and Ethel and then straightened, narrowing his brown gaze on me. "How are you doing, Joey?"

I gave him a smile I hoped looked sincere. "I'm fine."

His eyes narrowed further and I sighed.

"Really. The nightmares are almost gone." Not really.

He winced and I laughed. "I'm just teasing. I'm actually doing okay."

"Good." Arno shook Hal's hand. "How's the shoulder?"

Hal had dived behind the rusted-out harvester when Pru and Arno had started shooting at him that night in the lot. He had a pretty nasty bruise on his shoulder from smacking up against the sharp edge of the massive implement. But, with bullets flying around everywhere, he was lucky to have escaped with only a bruise.

He lifted his arm and rolled it. "Almost as good as new."

"I'm really sorry, man..."

"Please, no more apologies. There's no way you could have known."

Arno put his hands on his narrow hips and

looked at his boots, sighing. "I'm just glad the plan worked. Mostly."

It hadn't been in the plan for Polly to grab the bag of money while Hal had been getting fired on. But the tracker they'd inserted into the middle of one of the stacks of bills had worked like a charm.

I'd learned after the Feds and Arno, with Hal riding shotgun, had come roaring to my rescue, that Pru's guys had spotted Polly going for the money and had let her go. They'd followed her to the river road and lost her when she'd apparently found the tracker and gotten rid of it. No doubt at Angie's suggestion.

But they'd been nearby when I'd called. Fortunately, Hal had returned the blind call from the burner.

"I still can't believe Medford was there," Hal said, eyeing Arno carefully.

I'd noticed him doing that a lot over the last few days, as if he thought Arno knew something important he wasn't telling us.

Arno cleared his throat and looked away, all but confirming Hal's suspicion.

"Has he been arrested?" I asked.

Arno shook his head. "We have no proof that he was there."

"You have my word."

"I do," Arno nodded. "But Medford has the best

lawyers money can buy. Your word wouldn't get us through the door. Nothing personal."

I scrunched up my face. "But it *is* personal, isn't it, Arno? It's very personal. And I hate that he got the money."

Hal and Arno shared a grin.

"What?"

"He got a few hundred dollars. The first bill in every stack was real. The rest were blanks," Arno said.

I laughed.

"Medford's sharp. He would have known we'd give him empties. He must have taken the bag for a different reason," Arno said, frowning thoughtfully.

Whatever the reason he was there, Medford had certainly taken the opportunity to lie to me again about my mother. Though, looking back on that night, I couldn't deny that he'd seemed sincere.

"Pru says Angie Lucklin isn't talking," Arno went on. "They've matched the casings at the auction lot to her rifle, and the slug we pulled out of the tree at the trailer to a 22 she owns, but there's no evidence to place her at the scene of Hadley's murder. Pru thinks she can get Mrs. Lucklin to talk by offering her a deal for a shorter sentence."

"You have Joey's statement," Hal reminded him.

Arno nodded. "That will help, but I'd rather have a confession."

"You believe the story she told me, about who

actually killed Lucky?"

"It fits the evidence," Arno said. "And the motive seems right. Hadley no doubt killed Lucky for the money. Polly's role in all of it is a question mark. She may or may not have been involved in killing Lucky. But she was definitely working with Angie to find the money after he was dead."

"Lucky didn't even tell his girlfriend where he hid it?" I asked. "Cold."

"Yeah, but it turns out he had good instincts on that. They did end up killing him," Hal said.

I shrugged.

Arno's gaze slid to mine. "Polly's system had a large dose of blood-thinner in it. We found a bottle of the same thinner at Angie Lucklin's house, with her late husband Lyle's name on the bottle. Angie must have given it to her at some point and then left her to die. She literally bled out from the knife wound she got at the trailer."

I couldn't help remembering what Angie had told me about medicines proving useful.

"Can you prove that Angie attacked Polly at the trailer?" I asked.

"We can," Arno said. "We found the knife Angie used to attack Polly. It was buried in the woods by her farmhouse. We haven't been able to pull prints off of it yet, but we sent it to the Joliet Forensic Science Laboratory. They've got some of the country's best latent print examiners."

"It must have been quite a surprise when Polly showed up at the Lucklin's house," Hal said.

"Yeah," Arno said, shaking his head. "How's that for irony. She went to Lucky's mom for help after the woman tried to kill her."

"I'm surprised that Angie didn't finish the job right then and there," I said.

"She probably would have, but Polly no doubt explained to her at that point that there was a whole lot of money involved. Angie probably saw an opportunity to get some recompense for losing her son."

"I'll give you irony," Hal said. "If that girl had just stayed at the hospital either of the two times we sent her there, she probably would have been all right. We might have figured out Mrs. Lucklin had killed Pim and attacked Polly and had her in jail long before Polly even got out of the hospital."

"Apparently, all she could think about was the money," Arno said, sighing.

"One thing's been bothering me," I told the men. "Polly said they drove the Town Car to Deer Hollow. But how did Lucky's car get here?"

"Lucky drove the Chevy down himself. Aside from the owners' prints we only found Hadley's fingerprints in the Town Car. No prints from Lucky or Polly. She lied about Lucky stealing that car, probably to cover for her brother."

We stood in silence for a long moment, each of

us lost in our thoughts. Then Arno tapped his hat against his thigh. "I'll get out of your hair." He looked around. "You're really going to do this, huh? Sell your folks' business?"

I glanced toward the two closed office doors. Behind them were decades-worth of memories that I wasn't looking forward to stirring up. "I am. It's time."

Arno did something that surprised me a lot. He walked over and gave me a quick hug. "Let me know if you need help with anything. Anything at all."

Tears blurred my gaze at his unaccustomed kindness. "Thanks. I will."

He headed for the door, stopping with his hand on the knob. "Let's do something together soon...the four of us."

I grinned, and Arno returned it. With everything that had happened over the last few days, it hadn't really hit me until that moment. "We have our girl back," I told him.

He laughed, his gaze sparking with pleasure. "We do. And she's already hitting me up to sell my house."

I laughed at that. "Lis is going to be a great realtor."

Hal dropped his arm around my shoulders, kissing me on top of the head. "I might have some business for her soon," he said, causing me to frown.

Shock made my eyes go wide. "You're selling the cabin?"

His grin was enigmatic. He winked at me, and the combo of the knee-melting smile and the wink should have distracted me. They probably would have if his words hadn't both warmed and alarmed me.

What in the world was going on in that delicious brain of his?

And when in the world was he going to fill me in?

If he was tempted to tell me, he didn't get the chance. Arno opened the door just as a squirrel bounded past outside, a mere five yards from the office building.

With a single, delighted bark, Caphy was off and running, nearly taking Arno off his feet on her way through the door.

Though she wouldn't have any idea what to do with a squirrel unless it was skinned, cooked, and placed neatly into a bowl for her, Ethel Squeaks squealed her delight of the chase and took off after my pitty.

The chase was on.

And, as always, I was pulling up the rear.

Story of my life.

The End

READ MORE COUNTRY COUSIN MYSTERIES

If you enjoyed **Unlucky Bumpkin**, you might want to check out the rest of the series. Please enjoy Chapter One of **Humpty Bumpkin**, Book 1 of the *Country Cousin Mysteries* as my gift to you!

———————

She's just a country girl who loves her dog. But her life is about to get less countrified and more...erm...homicide.

Deer Hollow is a small community built in a verdant, rolling countryside. The nearest big city is over an hour away, and big city ways are rejected at the Hollow. Unfortunately, the big city isn't the only place where bad things can happen.

Things like murder...which has a funny way of

messin' up a debutante's day and turning a sunny Sunday in June right over onto its bucolic head.

HUMPTY BUMPKIN

The whole communication revolution thing is a mixed bag of wonderful and tedious. Things like cell phones are a revelation, allowing twenty-something women like me, who have trouble sitting still, to stay in touch with the important people in their lives while we go about our business.

But even the best innovations have their downside.

For example, a wise woman once told me never to answer a phone call whose number you don't recognize. *Answer at your own risk*, my cousin Felicity proclaimed one rainy day in the arboretum.

And I've since witnessed the intelligence of her advice. Several times over.

Unfortunately, I'm apparently a slow learner.

"Hello?"

"Is this Miss Joey Fulle?"

I frowned, not liking the "I want to sell you a bridge" tone of the caller's voice. "Nope, sorry. I think you have the wrong number."

"Actually, I believe I have the right number, Miss Fulle."

"You're not right," I said quickly and disconnected before the man on the other end of the phone had a chance to give me bad news. I had no idea what kind of bad news I was expecting. But I knew it was there, lurking like a vulture in a tree, ugly and ravenous.

I tugged the soft twisty off my shoulder-length red-blonde hair and reached up to smooth the hair back into my favorite style, which was a high ponytail. Sweat dripped down between my shoulder blades, and I was glad I'd dressed for the heat of an early June morning. Though my plain white tank top and cut off jean short shorts were already damp.

My dog, Cacophony, Caphy for short, bounded up and stopped in front of me, a clump of fur between her jaws. I grimaced. "Caphy, what did you do? Have you killed something again?"

A blonde Pitbull with gorgeous green eyes, Caphy bounced several times, her muscular haunches springing her several inches off the ground each time, and then barked happily and ran off again, tail whipping the air. I sighed, knowing I should follow her and see if I could save whatever she'd decided to "play" with.

My phone rang again. I hit *Ignore* and trudged after my dog. "Caphy girl, where'd you go?"

The distant sound of barking drew me to a copse of old trees, their gnarled branches bigger around than I was and tangled together high overhead. It was behind one of these, an elegant old Elm tree whose knobby arms spread wider than the rest, that my dog was mostly hidden. I could see her butt wagging happily as she moved around behind the tree.

"Caphy, come!"

My sweet Pitty bounced out from behind the distant tree and grinned at me, her entire body vibrating with excitement. "What have you found, girl?" I murmured to myself. "Come on, Caphy."

But she turned back to whatever she was exploring. That was when I realized she must have cornered something. I picked up the pace and hurried in her direction.

By the time I was fifteen feet away, I smelled something rotting and knew that, whatever she'd found, I wouldn't be saving it.

Real panic set in. "Caphy, you come here right now!"

My dog disappeared behind the tree, and I growled with frustration. But a moment later, she reappeared, heading in my direction with something hanging out of her mouth. "Ugh!" I fought an impulse to turn and run. Being corpse-woman was not tops on my list of favorite things.

In fact, I was pretty sure it wasn't on the list at all. "Drop it, Cacophony."

Of course she ignored me, her steps becoming bouncier and more excited the closer she came. Clearly, she wanted to share her treasure with me. I didn't know how to impress upon her that having a mangled, half-dried corpse of a bunny or squirrel dropped on my shoes didn't take me to my happy place. My usual response of shrieking and running screaming away from her treasure just didn't seem to be doing much to teach her.

She was a very bull-headed pitty. I grinned at my pun.

Caphy ran up and dropped to her haunches a few feet away. She kept hold of the object, which I was trying hard not to look at, as if she was afraid I was going to take it away from her. She would be right about that. But it wasn't going to happen until I had a bag or something to use so I didn't have to touch it. I tried one more time to get her to let loose of whatever she was clutching between her jaws. "Drop it, girl." If I was really lucky, I could convince her to let go of it and I could drag her home.

To my shock, she lowered her head and released the contents of her mouth.

I glanced down. My stomach did a painful little dance, and my gag reflex kicked in. Caphy was watching me very carefully, letting the object lie there as if checking to see how I would react. I was glad it was out of her mouth.

In fact, I would have been elated about it.

But I was too busy shrieking and running away. It might not work for her...but it worked just fine for me.

Deputy Arno Willager peered toward the object hulking under the trees. Two, skinny white stick-like things protruded from one end, their bony lengths painted in red streaks. He narrowed his dark brown gaze at the thing, no doubt gawking at the enormous feet on the end of the sticks.

I shuddered beside him, my dog vibrating excitedly next to me on a leash.

"Is this your chipper, Joey?"

I gave him the full force of my hostile blue gaze. "Uh, no, Deputy Willager. It's not my chipper. And, before you ask, that's not my body either."

He lifted a golden eyebrow and quirked wide lips as he skimmed my own personal body a long, slow look. "Oh, I can see that."

I frowned but didn't scold him for giving me the once over. I was on uneven ground with that one because I was pretty sure there'd been one time at a party in high school when I'd been in a closet with

Arno, our star quarterback at the time. We'd been pretty drunk and the details of what we'd been doing in there were vague. I decided that changing the subject might be a good idea. "Do you know..." I swallowed hard. "—who it is?"

Arno wrinkled his nose. "Can't be more than a couple people around here with feet that big."

I nodded, covering my nose with a hand as a warm breeze carried the butcher shop stench in our direction. "It's horrible."

Arno didn't respond. Finally, I looked at him. "Did you call Doctor Miller?"

"I did."

"Well, that's good." I glanced down at the item on the ground a few feet away. It was part of a hand. A man's hand if size was any indication. The ends of the fingers were missing, and my stomach roiled.

"Tell me how you found it."

"I told you already. "

"Humor me, Joey."

I sighed. "Caphy and I were taking a walk. It's a nice day."

He scoured me a look and I fought a grin. He was just too easy to annoy for his own good. "Caphy ran up ahead and came back with fur in her mouth."

"Fur?"

"Well...I thought it was fur. But clearly, it wasn't." My gaze skimmed to the small patch of scalp resting in the dirt where Caphy had dropped it.

"Did you walk up to the chipper?"

"No."

"You didn't touch anything? Move the body parts...?"

"Ew! Of course not. Why would you even ask me that?"

"It's my job."

Frustration twanged my last nerve. Arno had always been a man of few words, but he had to know I had about a thousand questions. As if reading my mind, he turned to frown down at me. The sun dropped slowly behind him, forming a backdrop for his tall, lean frame, narrow hips and broad shoulders. Arno's face was classically handsome, with a clean-shaven square jaw, sexy brown eyes and a pleasantly-shaped mouth with a slightly fuller lower lip that was immensely appealing. Two lines rode the space between his dense golden brows as he looked at me. He was clearly chewing on something he thought he should tell me.

"What is it, Arno?"

The worry lines deepened and he held my gaze with a searching one. "You can't talk about this, Joey. This is an ongoing investigation and I need you to promise me you won't spill details around town."

"I don't know any details."

"You know more right now than anybody else except the killer." He lifted a golden brow for emphasis.

His words finally sank in. "Oh. Yikes."

"I need you to keep a low profile until we figure out what's going on."

"Surely, this is someone from outside the *Hollow*."

He shrugged. "We don't know that yet."

I fell silent, chewing my bottom lip as a distant rumbling noise climbed ever closer to the spot where we stood. That would be Doctor Miller and the deputies Arno had called. They would have left their cars on the road and were approaching on all-terrain vehicles. My family's property included well over a hundred acres without roads. And the spot where Arno and I stood was in the most remote section of it all. The killer couldn't have found a more private spot to stick some poor schmoe into a wood chipper.

Finally, I nodded. "Okay. I promise."

"Good. Now you should get on home with that dog. She's disrupted the crime scene enough."

Caphy whined softly and dropped to her wide haunches, plying the deputy with a grin and soft eyes for good measure.

She wrung a grin out of him and he reached out to scratch the wide spot between her eyes. "You're a good girl, Caphy."

My pitty leaped to her feet and started wagging from her nose to the deadly whip of her tail, which unfortunately was smacking painfully against my leg.

I gave her leash a tug and, with one final look at the horror between the trees, we started back toward home. Despite my promise to keep the body in the chipper to myself, I had no intention of doing it. Whoever that poor soul was, he or she was killed on my property.

That made it personal.

And, personally, I didn't like it when people started flinging other people into wood chippers in my woods.

It was rude and disturbing.

And nipping it in the bud as quickly as possible seemed like the logical thing to do.

Check out the entire series here: https://samcheever. com/books/#Country

ALSO BY SAM CHEEVER

If you enjoyed **Unlucky Bumpkin,** you might also enjoy these other fun mystery series by Sam. To find out more, visit the **BOOKS** page at www. samcheever.com:

Country Cousin Mysteries **(More fun with Joey and Caphy!)**
Gainfully Employed Mysteries
Honeybun Heat Series
Silver Hills Cozy Mysteries
Yesterday's Paranormal Mysteries
Reluctant Familiar Paranormal Mysteries
Enchanting Inquiries Paranormal Mysteries

DON'T MISS OUT

Stay up on all Sam's news by joining her newsletter, and get a copy of a fun mystery just for signing up!

SIGN UP HERE!

ABOUT THE AUTHOR

Multiple-time USA Today and Wall Street Journal Best-selling Author Sam Cheever writes mystery and suspense, creating stories that draw you in and keep you eagerly turning pages. Known for writing great characters, snappy dialogue, and unique and exhilarating stories, Sam is the award-winning author of 80+ books.

To learn more about Sam and her work, visit her at one of her online hotspots:
www.samcheever.com
samcheever@samcheever.com